MELONHEAD

AND THE
VEGALICIOUS DISASTER

ALSO BY KATY KELLY

MELONHEAD

AND THE
VEGALICIOUS DISASTER

BY KATY KELLY

ILLUSTRATED BY GILLIAN JOHNSON

DELACORTE PRESS

Text copyright © 2012 by Katy Kelly
Jacket art and interior illustrations copyright © 2012 by Gillian Johnson

Visit us on the Web! randomhouse.com/kids
Educators and librarians, for a variety of teaching tools, visit us at RHTeachersLibrarians.com

Library of Congress Cataloging-in-Publication Data
Kelly, Katy.
Melonhead and the vegalicious disaster / by Katy Kelly ; illustrated by Gillian Johnson. — 1st ed.
p. cm.
Summary: Can Adam "Melonhead" Melon, who lives in the Washington, D.C., neighborhood of Capitol Hill, survive his fearsome fifth-grade teacher and his mother's resolution to cook healthy, nutritious meals?
ISBN 978-0-385-74164-4 (hardcover) — ISBN 978-0-375-99015-1 (library binding) — ISBN 978-0-375-98667-3 (ebook) [1. Behavior—Fiction. 2. Food—Fiction. 3. Teachers—Fiction. 4. Washington (D.C.)—Fiction. 5. Humorous stories.] I. Johnson, Gillian, ill. II. Title.
PZ7.K29637Mi 2012
[Fic]—dc23
2011049429

Printed in the United States of America

10 9 8 7 6 5 4 3 2 1

First Edition

For Max Kelly,
who came to me as a sister-in-law and became my sister.
Thank you for making my books and my life better.

1

THE HORRIBLE DAY

"Are you excited, Sport?" my dad asked.

"Nervous?" my mom said. "Anxious?"

"Ready to be a fifth grader?" my dad asked.

"I'd rather be stuck in quicksand with chirping crickets stuck in both ears," I said.

My mom yelped, "How would crickets get in your ears?"

"By jumping," I said.

"Adam, don't ever let crickets jump into your ears," my mom said. "I mean it."

My dad poured her coffee.

"Only half a cup," she

said. "I'll have more at the Second Annual First-Day-of-School All-You-Can-Eat Eggstravaganza."

"I can't believe they sprung Ms. Madison on us," I said. "With a one-day warning."

"Life changes, Sport," my dad said. "We adjust."

"Lucy Rose says the principal should not have let Mrs. George retire," I told them. "Especially since Jonique has been waiting her whole life to be in Mrs. George's class. Ms. Madison should stay in middle school where she belongs. You can't just walk into a classroom and take over."

"You can if the principal hires you to teach fifth grade," my dad said.

"Young teachers are fun teachers," my mom said. "The letter said we're lucky to get her."

"Kids call her Bad Ms. Mad," I said.

"I'm sure that's a friendly nickname, just like Melonhead," my mom said. "Your friends don't think you have a melon for a head."

"Melonhead is an honor for our last name," I said. "It's a compliment. Bad Ms. Mad is the truth. People do think I have a head like a melon. Pop said I have the roundest head he's ever seen on a ten-year-old boy."

Pop's the inventor of the Eggstravaganza and also my old friend. His wife, Madam, is too, only she's not as old. Their granddaughter, Lucy Rose, is my same-age friend.

"Pop said your head was too round?" my mom said.

"Betty," my dad said. "Adam has a fine head. We Melons are proud of our heads."

"Pop said I need the extra brain space," I said.

"That's true," my mom said. "You are exceptionally smart. Pop is right."

"Exactly," my dad said. "I read that fifth grade is a time of great growth."

"For heads?" my mom said.

"For judgment and responsibility," he said.

"Is that true?" my mom asked.

"It could be," he told her. "I believe our boy could be the leader of the pack."

"Do you mean pack like a pack of wolves?" I asked.

My dad laughed and crumpled my new haircut with his hand.

"Daddy meant pack like a pack of gum," my mom said. "Quiet, contained, and just like the other gum in your class."

"I should be gumlike?" I asked.

"Just don't be wolflike," she said. "I don't enjoy getting calls from Mr. Pitt."

"They're worse for the person he's calling about," I said.

"Well, I hope Daddy's right. You are my Darling Boy, but a dose of judgment would help me worry less. I've barely slept since the Great Glue Incident."

"The GGI was one hundred percent accident," I said. "It could happen to anybody with hair."

"Let's not replay yesterday," my dad said. "Our boy learns from his mistakes, don't you, Sport?"

"It is amazing how much I've learned," I said.

Sometimes my dad laughs for no reason.

My mom unzipped a plastic bag. "Carrots, celery, or both?" my mom asked. "For lunch."

"None of the above," I said.

"Dr. Stroud said you need more vegetables."

"He said I need more green, yellow, and red in my diet," I told her. "I'm already doing it. By drinking more Gatorade."

"Dr. Stroud meant red, green, and yellow vegetables," my mom said. "Starting today you'll be eating more of them."

I made my famous throwing-up sound.

"I told Dr. Stroud that was our New School Year's resolution," she said. "And we're sticking to it."

If I hadn't been in such a rush to get to the Eggstravaganza, my brain alarm would have gone off.

2

THE SECOND ANNUAL FIRST-DAY-OF-SCHOOL ALL-YOU-CAN-EAT EGGSTRAVAGANZA

The minute my skateboard turned the corner, everybody on Madam and Pop's front porch started clapping.

My ace friend, Sam Alswang, was standing on the bench swing. Gumbo the giant black poodle was in the yard, running circles around Pop.

"It's about time, Frank N. Stein," Sam screamed.

It's lucky I heard him, because Mrs. Alswang was telling him to get down in a loud way. Lucy Rose was balancing on her stomach on top of the porch railing, acting like the Paul Revere of Washington, D.C. Only she was screaming, "The Melons are

coming! The Melons are coming!" Her top friend, Jonique McBee, was holding Lucy Rose by her red cowboy boots so she wouldn't fall overboard.

Sam's parents were waving their hands. Pop was waving his spatula. I felt like a hotshot.

I skateboarded through the gate screaming, "Thank you, Melonhead fans!" I took a rolling bow.

Going top speed on four wheels while you're bent in half, balancing your backpack, and holding a pickle jar full of beetles is harder than it looks.

I did a face-plant in Madam's rosebush.

My mom is fast-acting. It took her two point five seconds to leap across the yard, yank me out, and scream, "You're bleeding!" In another second she found her first-aid kit in her purse and started swabbing my face with ointment.

"Stand still, Adam," she said.

The more anxiety my mom has, the squeakier her voice gets. When she's super nervous her voice is so high it's like a dog whistle for people.

My dad and I said the same thing at the same time.

"It's only a scratch."

She was not calmed.

"Scratches can get infected, you know."

"The good news is the beetles are fine," Sam said.

"They had a soft landing," Pop said. "On my foot."

"What a load of luck," I said.

My mom had just finished sanitizing me when, out of the corner of my ear, I heard, "Aerial attack!"

Sam beaned me with a bacon bomb. Since he's going to be a major-league pitcher, he has sharp aim. His bomb bounced off my neck.

"Duck, Chuck," he said.

Sam's sister, Baby Julia, is a copycat. Actually, she's a copydog. She's been acting doggish for three days. If you call her Julia she barks and says, "I Fifi."

Fifi-Julia stuck her hands through the railing and dropped four bacon bombs. I don't know if all babies are squeezers, but she is.

I raked the b-bombs up with my fingers and shoved them in my mouth.

My mom got to me before my first chew.

"Adam!" she said. "Small bites. Do you want me to have to do the Heimlich maneuver on you again?"

The H.M. is how you save a choking person. You hug them from behind and sock them in their gut. Food flies out of their windpipe. My mom Heimlichs me a lot. I have never been actually choking at the time.

Lucy Rose's mom called down from the porch. "I'm making Straw Man smoothies."

"That's short for strawberry-mango," Lucy Rose said. "Plus it comes with a straw."

"We brought Betty's famous eggs," my dad said.

"They're not really famous," my mom said. "Just well known."

"Ralph made ham biscuits," Mrs. Alswang said.

Mr. McBee held up a light blue box and said, "Cinni-minis from Baking Divas." He gets them for free. Mrs. McBee is a Diva.

"This is one delicious porch party," Sam said.

"Porch funeral," I said.

"Who died?" Mr. Alswang asked.

"Fun," Sam said.

"Joy," Jonique said.

"In forty-two minutes, happiness will be a thing of the past," Lucy Rose said. "Like typewriters."

"Goodbye, good life," I said. "Rest in peace."

"This is a grave situation," Mr. Alswang said.

Graves are nothing to joke over, but all the adults laughed.

3

THE PORCH FUNERAL

Sam tried to break the glumness by saying, "I hear some people enjoy Ms. Madison."

"In the entire history of Ms. Madison, not one person has enjoyed her," I said. "Believe me."

"Believe him," Sam told his dad. "Elizabeth Wilson says Ms. Mad gives *four* hours of homework *every* night. Extra if the class isn't cooperating."

"Could Elizabeth Wilson be exaggerating?" my dad asked.

"Not at all," Lucy Rose said. "Elizabeth is an excellent-O judge of teachers on account of in middle school she had Mrs. George, who is utterly

divine. I say if you can judge greatness, you can also judge terribleness."

"How bad is Mad?" Pop asked.

"She makes people *recopy*," Jonique said.

"But I do that anyway."

"Julianne Meany says Ms. Mad flunks people," I said. "One mistake and it'll be hello, fifth grade again."

"She's mean in the extreme," Lucy Rose said. "Last year, she wouldn't let the Dunkleburger triplets sit together. I say if you are born together you should get to sit together."

"Trip Pate told me that when Wilson Tibbits didn't stop playing with the window shade that very instant, Ms. Mad went berserk," Sam said.

"She had zero sympathy when the roller flew off and stabbed him in the head," Lucy Rose said.

"You have to Stay On Task even if your head is cracked and your brains are gushing," I said.

"Whose head was cracked and gushing?" my mom said. When she's in alarm mode her words sound like they're splattering.

"No one's head," I said. "That was an example."

"A puny example," Lucy Rose said. "Ms. Mad forces kids to do child labor. Especially math."

"Why, she can't get away with that!" Pop said.

"She actually can," Jonique said.

"When Jonique and I were at Grubb's drugstore buying Pop toenail clippers for his birthday, Sally Ann Richardson said her breath smells like skunk," Lucy Rose said.

"Sally Ann should brush her teeth," Sam said.

"Sally Ann's breath smells like Chiclets," Lucy Rose said. "Jonique's talking about Ms. Mad's teeth."

"Why should Sally Ann brush Ms. Madison's teeth?" Pop asked. "If Ms. Madison is old enough to teach fifth grade, she is old enough to brush her own teeth."

That made everybody fall apart with wild hyena laughing.

"Ms. Madison can't be this awful," my mom said. "Can she?"

"Ms. Mad doesn't care a skink about human children," Lucy Rose said.

"Is *skink* your Word of the Day, Lucy Rose?" Madam asked.

"Yes," Lucy Rose said. "It means 'the puniest shred.'"

"I've never heard it before," Madam said.

"On account of I made it up," Lucy Rose said.

"That is some fine original thinking," Pop told her.

Mrs. Alswang passed the ham biscuits. I took three.

Mr. McBee smiled. "Every September students get Ms. Madaphobic. But all of them survive *and* learn to divide and multiply fractions and write a report."

"And dance the bossa nova," Pop said.

"There is no way I'm dancing," I said.

"We are doomed," Jonique said.

"D-Double-D-doomed," Lucy Rose said. "Utterly."

And then, all of a sudden, we weren't.

Four phones rang. Four parents answered, listened, and hung up.

"Recorded message," Sam's dad said.

"Gas leak," my dad said.

"In the school," Lucy Rose's mom said.

"Are they crazy?" my mom said. "Children should not be near gas leaks!"

I pretended to fart.

"Melonhead's leaking!" Sam yelled.

"It'll be fixed by tomorrow," Mrs. Alswang said.

Another phone rang. It was Jonique's mom, calling from her job at Baking Divas.

"School's canceled?" Jonique screamed.

"We're saved!" I shouted.

"One more day of summer!" Sam hollered.

Pop instantly made up a song called "Happy Days Are Here Again."

"I'm going to remember how a miracle feels," I said. Then I hooted all over the place.

Weird thing: Even though Jonique and Lucy Rose are anti–Ms. Mad, they were cranky that school got canceled.

"You two make negative zero sense," I said.

"There's no such thing as negative zero," Jonique said.

"You should be kissing the gas leak," I told Lucy Rose.

"Thanking it for your freedom," Sam said.

"We're prepared for today," Lucy Rose said. "We got twin school supplies."

"My back-to-school outfit is new today," Jonique said. "Tomorrow it will be used."

Lucy Rose pointed at her hair. "This is an utter waste of my new yellow bandana."

"It looks like your old yellow bandana," I said.

She rolled her eyeballs at me.

"How about we take your first-day-of-school pictures anyway?" Lucy Rose's mom said.

Jonique and Lucy Rose put their arms around each other's shoulders and held up their notebooks. They're covered with miniature dogs with huge eyes. The notebooks, not the girls. It would be more interesting if the girls were covered with big-eyed mini-dogs.

"You and Sam should get twin stuff," Lucy Rose said.

"Why?" I asked.

"So everyone will know you're best friends," she said.

"Why?" Sam asked.

"Smile and say, 'We're gorgeous,'" Lucy Rose's mom told them.

"Why do girls like to have proof of everything they do?" I asked Pop.

"That's one of life's mysteries," Pop said.

Sam looked at me. "We have no time for a photo, Moto."

"I'm reading your brain, Jane."

"Melonhead and I can't stay one second longer," Sam told Madam and Pop. "We have to cram the rest of summer into today."

The last thing we heard was Mrs. Alswang saying, "Julia! Do not bite Madam's ankle!"

4

THE LAST, LAST DAY OF SUMMER

Here's what Sam and I did.

1. Rode the elevator to the top of the Washington Monument. Counted to make sure there are fifty flags for fifty states. There are fifty-six. Reported the mistake to the gift shop lady. It turned out one flag is for Washington, D.C. Five are for territories. One is Puerto Rico. Another one's called Guam.

2. Went to the aquarium in the Commerce Building to look at the giant vinegaroons. We expected them to be over six feet tall. Found out six inches is giant for a vinegaroon. Here's how I'm

like a vinegaroon: we both have relatives in Florida. His are scorpions that live in the Everglades. Mine are grandparents who live in Boca Raton.

3. Got a free lollipop at the bank.

4. Ate triple-decker BLTs at my house. Gave Sam my tomato. Reloaded my cargo pants pockets with Golden Grahams and Joe's O's.

5. Had a hose fight.

6. Invented ice hats made out of sacks of frozen peas and string. Wore them around the neighborhood until they thawed. Rating: Magnificent.

7. Scooped cereal mush out of my pockets. It tasted okay.

8. Visited our ancient friend, Mrs. Wilkins, to report on vinegaroons and hint around for ice cream. I got pistachio. Sam picked lemon sorbet. For a gift we gave her one huge sack of unfrozen peas.

9. Took Julia for a walk on Gumbo's leash.

10. Did an experiment with Coca-Cola and Mentos.

11. Went to Mr. and Mrs. Good-neighbors' house.

12. Got sent home by Mrs. Alswang.

My mom and I were sweating and weeding the front yard when a taxi pulled up and my dad got out.

"Hello, Sport!" he said.

He usually walks because Congressman Buddy Boyd's office is across from the U.S. Capitol in Washington, D.C., and that's only a few blocks from our house. Dad plus cab means:

1. I'm in trouble.
2. Something is special.

Today's cab was a good one.

"I have to hear about the bonus last day of summer," he said.

"We're celebrating with meat loaf," my mom said.

When she leaned her cheek over for a kiss, my dad swirled her around and picked her up like she was a giant baby. He was so fast her sandal flew off.

"That's called sweeping a lady off her feet," he said.

"Ladies like that?" I asked my mom.

She laughed.

"They love it, Sport," my dad said. "Right, Betty?"

"Oh, we're mad for it," she said. "Now, put me down."

"Kiss me first," he said.

Gross.

"When you grow up you're going to be just as handsome as Daddy," my mom said. "And some girl is going to get just as lucky as I did."

Grosser.

"The Melon boys are Men of Style and Distinc-tion," my dad said.

"Let's get inside with the air-conditioning," my mom said.

"Wow!" my dad said. "It smells like magic in here."

I somersaulted past the hall table.

"The lamp!" my mom said.

Too late.

"Don't worry," I said. "I'm good at socking dents out of shades."

The dining room table had a blue cloth on it and candles. My mom fancies up when my dad gets to come home for dinner.

"Adam, you may carry out the unbreakables," my mom said.

I put the bread basket close to my plate for E-Z reaching. When I went back to the kitchen my mom was standing in front of the sink.

The delicious smell of meat mixed with salad dressing odors gave me a shocking idea.

I snuck up, grabbed my mom's waist with my right arm, tipped her with my knees, and lifted with one hundred percent of my might.

She let out screams of delight.

The next second it was raining lettuce.

"What are you doing?" she yelled. "Put me down!"

I dropped her fast.

My dad came rushing in. "What happened?"

"Adam frightened the life out of me," she said.

"You said ladies love being swept off their feet. And, Mom, you said *'mad for it.'* I had no way of knowing you were going to throw salad."

My mother got up and did a jig. I relaxed. Angry people don't dance.

It turned out to be because her foot landed in olive oil.

I was saving her but my dad jumped in my way.

"Grab my hand, Betty," he said.

We all hit the ground.

I was the only one laughing. You could tell they were cranky from the looks of their eyes.

"Parents," I said. "Breathe in. It smells just like vinegaroons in here."

"What?" my mom said.

"You know vinegaroons, Mom. They look like the kind of shining black bugs with exoskeletons that pop and crunch when you step on them, only they're actually arachnids. They attack by squirting acetic acid. You know what acetic acid is? Vinegar. The same thing that goes on salad. How cool is that?"

"Our vinegar comes from grapes," my mom said. "Not scorpions."

"It's a whip scorpion, *Mastigoproctus giganteus*," I said.

My dad knee-walked to the cabinet and unspun a roll of paper towels. After he rolled out pathways he gave my mom a wad.

"Betty," he said. "Your silk blouse."

"Your seersucker pants," she said.

"Your skirt, Mom," I said. "Look at her butt, Dad."

He looked at me instead.

"Come on, Parents," I said. "When you think about it, it's funny."

They have no humor.

"Cheer up," I said. "Silk is cheap."

"Cheap?" my dad asked.

"Sure," I said. "Silkworms work for free. People just collect and sew. Not like cotton. You have to grow and pick and put it in the gin."

"Gather the lettuce, Sport," he said.

"Back in the bowl, good as new," I said.

"Throw it in the disposal," my mom said.

"It's fine," I said. To prove it, I ate two croutons.

"Don't eat off the floor, Adam!" she said.

"Dad says our floors are clean enough to eat off of," I said.

"Not literally," my mom said.

She went downstairs to the laundry room and came back wearing blue shorts and a red T-shirt.

I thought she would have been more thankful to me for cleaning up the mess. Also to Dad for hauling dinner to the table.

My mom's rule is nobody can eat until everybody's

together. We had to sit and be tempted by meat loaf until my dad changed into his plaid shorts and squirted stain remover on his seersucker. By then my starvation had multiplied.

"I already called an end piece," I told him.

I took the glass top off a bowl. "Man-o-man alive!" I said. "Mashed potatoes with cheese sauce. It's like we're at Jimmy T's lunch counter! Thank you, Mom!"

My dad served her the first spoonful.

"I'll have a load of it, please," I said.

I had my fork ready to stab.

"Grace before dinner, Adam," my mom said.

"We are truly grateful for the food before us," I said as fast as I could.

My first bite was a mini-mountain. "The cheese is hot and melty," I said.

"Don't talk with your mouth full, Darling Boy," my mom said.

I spit it into my napkin.

"Adam, I meant swallow before you speak," she said.

"There's rot in it."

"Mine is tasty," my dad said.

"Well, the next bite will gag you to death," I told him. "Believe me. A spoiled, putrid potato got in with the good ones. Sorry, Mom. That's the second thing you made today that has to go in the garbage."

My mom took a bite.

"Parents, put down your forks," I said. "These could be killer potatoes. Jonique's dad did a report for the government on how many people die from eating decayed food. I don't know how many but it's a lot. The Melon family could be next."

"Well, that was a bust," my mom said.

"Don't blame yourself," I told her. "Bad potatoes are like head lice."

My mom turned pale.

"I mean they can happen to anybody. Even to a clean lady like you."

"No head lice talk at the table," my dad said.

My mom made a sigh. "Mrs. Mannix told me that not one of her children could tell the difference between mashed potatoes and mashed cauliflower."

I could not believe it. "My own mother made me lie to God," I said.

"I wouldn't do that," she said.

"You did," I said. "Because I am not truly grateful for this food. What I am is truly disgusted. And not in a good way."

My mom's lips stretched into a frown. Her neck bones made ridges. "We made a resolution," she said.

I didn't.

"Cauliflower isn't red or green or yellow," I said.

"Most white vegetables are starches," she said. "But not cauliflower. And it also comes in green, orange, and purple. I was planning to try a more colorful one next."

"No," I said.

"Try again, Sport," my dad said.

"No, thank you," I said.

"I meant try the cauliflower again," he said. "It's outstanding. It's just not what you expected."

I ate a forkful of contaminated sauce.

"Now, who says they don't like cauliflower?" he asked.

Me, that's who.

I only thought it.

To move the topic, I said, "This meat loaf is so good the president should serve it when kings visit."

They made me eat five bites of cauliflower mush. I gagged on every swallow.

Barf was in my throat. Or else it was the cauliflower.

Luckily, I remembered that ladies do not enjoy stories about vomit. Instead of the truth, I said, "I'm one hundred percent full."

"Okay," my mom said. "I'll try again tomorrow. We have to find vegetables you will eat."

"E-Z P-Z," I said. "Garlic bread and ketchup."

Even though garlic grows from the earth and

ketchup comes from tomatoes, she wouldn't count them.

I made a wish: *Please let this be a phase.*

"Any dessert?" my dad asked.

"Homemade brownies," my mom said.

"Now that's my kind of food," I said.

"The Mannix children never notice that they have spinach in them," my mom said.

"They must be the kind of kids who believe quarters come out of their ears," I said.

My dad washed the dishes while my mom practiced leaning backwards.

"Backache, Betty?" he asked.

"Being swept off my feet left my spine feeling twisted," she said.

"You think yours is twisted?" I said. "Try being the person who picks you up."

5

YOU CAN'T FAKE SICK ON THE FIRST DAY

Usually Sam and I pick Lucy Rose up on our way to school. But when her mom works late, Lucy Rose sleeps at Madam and Pop's. Then she comes to get me. We have a footpool. That's a carpool without a car.

She rang our bell and knocked and yelled through the mail slot at the same time. My dad answered. I was busy packing my pockets. My mom was busy giving me a talk about You Never Get a Second Chance to Make a First Impression.

"So if I'm a knucklehead today, Ms. Mad will think I'm a knucklehead every day?" I said.

"Exactly," my mom said. "I cannot have her thinking my Darling Boy is a knucklehead."

"Deal," I said. "But you remember that most trouble isn't permanent. Lots of situations turn out to be no harm, no foul, no reason to get upset."

"No harm?" my mom said. "What do you call shooting a liter of Coca-Cola through Mr. Goodneighbor's bedroom window?"

"An experiment," I said.

"That was a Think Before Doing opportunity for you and Sam," she said.

"We did," I said. "What we thought was putting Mentos in a liter of Coca-Cola would be brilliant. We did not think it would turn into a two-story geyser."

"That's what's called unforeseeable," Lucy Rose said.

"And when you think about it, it was lucky for the Goodneighbors," I said.

"Lucky?" my mom said.

"Very," I said. "They got free cleaning. We hosed off their window screen, mopped their floor, and washed their Exercycle. Plus we took their wet sweaters to Lustre Cleaners and shampooed their dog. In the end their stuff was cleaner than before we sprayed Coca-Cola on it."

"Jonique is waiting for us," Lucy Rose said. "And Sam."

"Have fun at school," my dad said.

"Have fun at recess," my mom said.

"Give Ms. Madison a chance," my dad said.

My mom followed us out the door. "Remember. Congress is back in session. Workers are back to stressing over laws they want to make and laws they want to throw out. And you know what stress leads to?"

"Careless driving," I said.

"Which means?"

"Be extra careful crossing streets," I said.

We have this conversation a lot. Only sometimes people are distracted by holidays or weather or tensions in the air.

"Come straight home after school," she said.

"Can he come to Baking Divas?" Lucy Rose asked. "Pop's treating. He wants to hear the ecstasies and the agonies of Day One."

"The whats?" I said.

"Ecstasy equals excellent-O," Lucy Rose said. "Agony is P-U."

"Expect a load of agonies," I said. "Ecstasies will be skink."

"See you after Pop's treat," my mom said.

Then she hugged me harder than when she's doing the Heimlich.

6

REPORTING ON DAY ONE

Pop was clipping Gumbo to the Baking Divas bike rack when we got there.

"Hail the conquering fifth graders!" he said. "You must be starving."

"Believe it," I said.

I shook the bakery door so the bell would ring a lot. "That's how Mrs. McBee knows it's us," I told Pop.

"We're here, Mom," Jonique said.

That's another way she knows.

Jonique's Aunt Frankie leaned over the cake case and said, "You're going to wear a hole in that bell, young man."

"I'm trying," I told her. "But so far I can't make a dent."

"Tell me about Ms. Madison, Sweet Pea," Mrs. McBee said. Sweet Pea is Jonique but everybody answered.

"Not the best," Sam said.

"Not the worst," Jonique said.

"Ms. Mad kept talking after the bell. We missed three minutes of recess," Sam said.

"I say that is a sign of poor teaching and rude inconsideration," Lucy Rose said.

"True," I said. "We would never ask her to teach us during recess."

"Holding you over for a few minutes is small potatoes," Mrs. McBee said.

"Or small cauliflowers," I said.

Sam, Jonique, and Lucy Rose laughed. They knew the whole sad story of the resolution. The grown-ups didn't get my humor.

"When I'm a teacher I will not be telling kids to do reports first thing," Jonique said.

"Ms. Mad did that?" Pop said.

"It's a biography of a Most Admired Person in History," Lucy Rose said.

"Ancient history? Modern history?" Mrs. McBee asked.

"Any time. As long as they're dead, they're history," Sam said.

"Most Admired Famous Dead Person," I said. "MAFDP for short."

"Are the bios due tomorrow?" Aunt Frankie asked.

"They're due in ten days," Jonique said.

Aunt Frankie blasted Pop's iced coffee with whipped cream.

"One Dulce Delicious cupcake, please," I said.

"A Peppermint Pinwheel, thank you," Sam said.

He's been stuck on them lately.

"We'd like two Smart Blondies," Jonique said. "Plus vanilla milks."

"Now you're eating matching food?" I said.

Aunt Frankie gave Pop the Cinni-mini with the most icing plus a dog snickerdoodle for Gumbo.

"May I take a number from the Now Serving machine?" I asked.

"No," Aunt Frankie said.

If she keeps saying no I am going to quit asking.

We sat outside at the table under the red umbrella.

"How was dreaded Ms. Mad?" Pop said. "Were her fangs showing?"

"She doesn't have fangs," Jonique said. "Just really large teeth."

"Three guesses what happened, Pop," Lucy Rose said.

"Ms. Madison poked you with sharpened toothpicks," Pop said.

Sam and I laughed like werewolves.

"It doesn't have to do with toothpicks," Jonique said.

Pop closed his eyes and held the top of his nose with two fingers. That is a sign of deep thinking.

"Ms. Madison made the class scrub the linoleum floors with eyebrow brushes."

"Eyebrow brushes?" Sam asked.

"Ladies use them to comb their eyebrows," Pop said.

I snorted.

"Is that a real thing?" Sam asked.

"It is," Pop said. "Madam doesn't leave the house with uncombed eyebrows."

"How big is an eyebrow brush?" I asked.

"A gerbil might use one as a toothbrush," Pop said. "But there shouldn't be any cross-species sharing. It's no good getting gerbil spit in your eyebrows."

We laughed like werewolves plus loons and baboons.

"Wrong again," Jonique said.

"About the floor scrubbing or the gerbils?" Pop asked.

"Both," Jonique said.

"Last guess," Lucy Rose said.

Pop's eyeballs bugged out like he was under zombie attack. His cheeks slouched. His mouth went straight. "Don't tell me Ms. Madison did the worst thing a teacher can do."

"Inside recess?" Sam said.

Pop shivered. "Inside recess is a holiday on ice compared to what I'm thinking of."

I know his worst thing.

"She didn't give us work sheets," I said.

"Excellent," Pop said. "Although they could be on order from Boring and Dullard Scholastic Supplies, Incorporated."

He is the funniest grown-up alive.

"Other than homework, what awful, unfair things did Ms. Madison inflict on your class?" Pop asked.

Lucy Rose smiled.

"Nothing," she said.

"Nothing at all," Jonique said.

"I was told that was impossible," Pop said. "People say she's an ogre. And by people I mean all of you."

Nobody answered.

"Surely she bellowed," Pop said.

"If that's the same as yelling, she didn't," Sam said.

"Gnashed her teeth?" Pop said.

"She sent Bart Bigelow to the Reflecting Table to reflect for booger flicking," I said.

"The Reflecting Table?" Pop said.

"If you're thinking it's made of mirrors, you're wrong as can be," Lucy Rose said. "It's blue wood. Ms. Mad says serene colors help people think about what they did wrong."

You could tell Pop was disappointed.

"She did admit that she's insane," Jonique said.

"Explain," Pop said.

"For summer vacation she rode a burro down to the bottom of the Grand Canyon," Jonique told him.

"On one side is rock," Lucy Rose said. "On the other side, there's nothing but air. In some places the path is so skinny that it's as wide as the burro."

"Halfway down's when she got the insanity," Jonique said.

Sam said, "Ms. Mad said, 'I looked down and I

thought I must be insane to trust this donkey not to fall off the edge.'"

"That's not loony," I said. "It would be loony if she had the chance and didn't go."

"I say it's very insane," Lucy Rose said. "Donkeys are not the smartest."

"Did she turn around?" Pop asked.

"It's not wide enough," Jonique said. "Plus, other people were coming behind her. If she turned she'd cause a burro jam."

"Also, she wanted to stay at the hotel at the bottom of the canyon," Lucy Rose said.

"Are you telling me that Ms. Mad is interesting?" Pop asked.

"When she's talking about the Grand Canyon," Sam said. "Not so interesting when she's talking about How to Study Effectively."

"So she has one good quality," Pop said.

"Two," I said. "She doesn't watch over me all day. That's due to my tip-top first impression."

"She didn't notice when Melonhead paper-clipped his eyelids," Lucy

Rose said. "But once the new kid is an old kid, she will."

"That is the honest truth," Jonique said. "Teachers focus on the new kids in the beginning. They're extra nice, to create comfort. But it goes away fast. Except it won't with me. When I'm a teacher I am always going to be extra nice."

"When I was new, Mr. Welsh stuck on me like glue," I said. "That lasted for the whole year."

"Pip is mature," Lucy Rose said.

"Pip?" Pop said.

"Pip Pinsky," Lucy Rose said. "She's excellent-O. Also a palindrome."

Palindromes are words that are spelled the same forward and backward. Lucy Rose collects them. Pop likes them. Probably because he is one.

"Everybody likes Pip," Sam said. "Except Ashley."

"And Marisol," Lucy Rose said. "On account of Ashley said if Marisol was Pip's friend, Ashley would cut their friendship. Ashley is jealous in the extreme."

"Because Pip got put in the front row," Sam said.

"I always get front row," I said.

"The behaved kids that deserve to be picked never are," Jonique said. She is behaved.

"Every time Ms. Mad looked at Ashley she got sour lips," Lucy Rose said.

"Ashley, not Ms. Mad," Jonique said. "That would create anti-comfort."

"At recess, Ashley told everybody that Pip is a teacher's pet," Lucy Rose said. "She's trying to get Pip ostrich-sized."

"Ostracized?" Pop asked.

"Ostrich-sized means no one will be your friend," Lucy Rose said. "It's my Word of the Day for tomorrow."

Pop smiled. He's proud of her W.O.D.s.

"Ashley might be trying to ostrich-size me," I said. "During Ms. Mad's talk called Fifth Graders Lead By Example, she interrupted and said, 'Melonhead is talking and Pip is answering.'"

"So Ms. Mad swung you around by your ankles?" Pop said.

"I wish. She said, 'As fifth graders, we do not

tattle, Ashley.' I wanted to say, 'Up your nose with a rubber hose, Ashley.' But I didn't."

"A wise choice for a boy trying to make an impression," Pop said.

"That's what I thought," I said.

"Then Ms. Mad said, 'We resolve our differences by talking. Ashley, tell Adam why his talking bothers you,'" Lucy Rose told Pop.

"Ashley fake-smiled at Melonhead," Jonique said.

"She sneered," Lucy Rose said.

"She was sneering?" I asked.

"No offense, Melonhead, but you are not the best at catching on," Lucy Rose said.

Jonique told the rest. "Ashley said, 'Adam, Ms. Madison has many important things to teach us. I want to hear them.'"

"Ms. Mad was fooled by that annoying girl," Lucy Rose said. "But Pip wasn't. I could tell from her eye rolls."

"I see Ashley is still Ashley," Pop said.

"She has not changed one skink of a speck," Lucy Rose said.

7

PIP, PIP, HOORAY!

On the walk home Sam said, "Tell Pop what Pip said, Fred."

"You tell, Mel."

"Pip thinks Melonhead and I are super hilarious," Sam said.

"At lunch I pretended to get my foot stuck in our classroom trash can," I said. "Only I acted like I didn't know I stepped in it. So I walked around saying, 'Who's making all this noise?' Then I tripped on purpose."

"He landed on his butt and rolled under

Robinson Gold's desk," Sam said. "It tipped sideways."

"Then I screamed, 'Who put this trash can on my foot?'"

"The whole class was laughing and clapping," Lucy Rose said. "Except Ashley."

"You can't complain about a teacher who lets you roll around with a trash can," Pop said.

"Ms. Mad was in the teachers' lounge," Jonique told him. "But the lunch aide said Melonhead should be a professional comedian."

"To top it off, Sam and I did our imitation of Mr. Pitt," I said. "I made my voice manly and wagged my finger and said, 'Melting crayons on the radiator in the boys' bathroom is inappropriate.'"

"Sam, do your Mr. Pitt," Lucy Rose said.

"'Putting plastic forks in your nose is dangerous and unsanitary,'" Sam said.

I went back to my Pitt voice and said, "'The classroom is not a carnival fun house.'"

"I wonder if Mr. Pitt ever regrets not going into the peat moss business," Pop said.

"Pip told us we crack her up," Sam told Pop.

"She's a laugh-a-lot girl," Lucy Rose said.

"She has sparkle eyes and style," Jonique said.

"More style than me?" Lucy Rose asked.

"The same amount," Jonique said.

I just figured out a Rule of Girls: *Never say anybody is better than your best friend, even if it is about a useless thing like style.*

"Red hair is better than blond hair," Jonique said.

Red is what Lucy Rose has.

"Black hair is fabulinity," Lucy Rose told her.

"Thank you," Jonique said.

"Hair can be a fleeting thing," Pop said. He has a bald patch.

"At her old school, Pip was the star of *Annie*," I said. "I told her, 'Pip, extreme talent is a thing we have in common.'"

"Only three kids are in the top math cluster," Jonique said. "One is Pip. Another one is me."

"Any thoughts on Pip?" Pop asked me.

I gave two thumbs-up. "Even though she didn't see our invention, she agrees that Sam and I should have won first prize at the Reinvention Fair. We are going to invent her a wheelchair that slides up and down stairs," I said.

"Pip uses a wheelchair?" Pop asked.

"It's neon blue with silver racing stripes," Sam said.

"On the back it has a sticker that says Eat Bertha's Mussels," Lucy Rose said.

"Mussels the seafood, not muscles in people," I said. "Pip says Bertha's is a restaurant in Baltimore."

"It has secret arm compartments," Sam said.

Pop looked confused. "The restaurant has arms?"

"Her chair has arms. They open up. She can stash stuff inside," Sam said. "But when Pip's on the move, her chair arms flip up. Otherwise they'd get in the way of her own arms when she's spinning her wheels."

"The chair arms are not all that secret," I said. "Our compartments will be invisible to the naked eyes."

"Aren't all eyes naked?" Jonique said.

"Melonhead asked Pip if having a wheelchair is fun," Lucy Rose told Pop.

"What did she say?" he asked.

"She asked me, 'Is walking fun?' I said, 'Running is fun. Walking is just how I get places. It's not a thing you think about.' She said, 'Same for wheelchairs. But racing is fun. So is popping wheelies.'"

"Pip's chair has little wheels on the back," Sam said. "She spins around, gets her speed up, and jerks back hard. Just like you do when you're on a bike."

"The big wheels tip up and all the balance goes to the puny back wheels," Lucy Rose said.

"Pip's got crazy-good skills," Sam said. "She won a third-place medal for racing in Aspen, Colorado."

"It is not easy to win medals in Colorado," Lucy Rose said.

"I wouldn't think so," Pop said. "Pip sounds like a pip."

"Oh, she is," Jonique said. "Even with teachers. Today when Ms. Mad said, 'I need a volunteer to get Pip's lunch out of her locker,' Pip raised her hand and said, 'I volunteer.'"

"Ms. Mad turned as red as my boots," Lucy Rose said. "Then Pip told Ms. Mad, 'If I can't do something I'll ask somebody.' And Ms. Mad said, 'That's what I'm here for.' So Pip said, 'Thanks but I don't need much help. Except with spelling.'"

"Well, Pip, Pip, Hooray!" Pop said. "Good for her."

8

UNEXPECTED DISGUSTINGNESS

I was taking off my shoes in the vestibule when I smelled something delicious. When I opened the door, I nearly fainted from joy.

"Mom," I yelled. "What's for dinner?"

"Pizza," she yelled back.

Usually I think everything is going to be great and somehow something goes wrong. Today I thought everything was going to be terrible and it turned out to be decent and now it was turning great. My mom is a pizza genius.

I threw my backpack on the hall bench, yelled, "Yabba dabba doo," and did my hooting dance down the hall and through the dining room.

"Hello, Mommo," I said.

"Hello, Darling Boy," she said.

"Dad! You're home for dinner again?"

"I couldn't wait to hear about Ms. Mad," he said. "Thumbs up or down?"

"Thumb sideways," I said. "Moving up."

"Pizza's ready," my mom said.

"And salad," my dad said.

"The pizza is a beauty," I  said.

And a relief.

It didn't taste beautiful.

"What's on this?" I asked.

"Toppings," my mom said.

"They're underneathings," I said. "The cheese is hiding something."

"Soybeans hardly have any taste," she said. "And they're a vegetable and a protein."

"I like the crust," my dad said. "It's different."

"Whole grain flour," my mom said.

"Can we go back to our old food?" I asked.

"Sweetie, this is our old food. I modernized it," she said. "And no, we can't stop. Dr. Stroud said a boy your age needs three cups of vegetables and two cups of fruit every day."

"How about I double up on fruit?"

"We made a resolution," she said.

I thought I was agreeing to Gatorade.

I dragged my teeth over the top to rake off cheese and sauce. It didn't work. Soy is a clingy bean. So I put my teeth in reverse, plowed the toppings back, and ate the crust.

When I'm quiet it makes my mom think I'm sad. "Did Ms. Mad frighten you, Darling Boy?" she asked.

"No," I said. "And can you just call me DB?"

"Great," she said. "It will be like a secret code between us."

I don't really want a secret mother/boy code.

"Ms. Mad's okay, then?" my dad asked.

"She's okay," I said. "Only she doesn't take Personal Responsibility."

"That's terrible," my mom said.

"What did she do?" my dad asked.

"Remember when I skimped on picking up the family room? You were disappointed because I dumped my Personal Responsibility?" I asked.

"That's when I made the chore wheel," my mom said.

"Ms. Mad is a skimper," I said.

My mom put her hand on my dad's arm. "We have to set up a conference," she told him. "A child as smart as Adam needs a full education."

"How does Ms. Mad skimp, Sport?" he asked.

"It's a known fact that telling kids to do homework is the teacher's responsibility, right?" I said.

My mom nodded. "You can't guess what she's thinking."

"Well," I said. "Ms. Mad *refuses* to remind people when a project is due."

"Refuses?" my dad asked.

"She will say it one time. Period. Forget and it's off to the Reflecting Table."

My dad laughed.

"I say the person who wants the homework should be the reminder. I should not be blamed for not being reminded."

My mom agreed. "Fifth grade is awfully young to have to keep track of everything."

"Sorry, Sport. That is your Personal Responsibility, not hers."

"I'll remind you when it's due, DB," my mom said.

"Betty," my dad said. "Adam can do this."

"We'll get you a homework calendar," my mom said.

Worst gift of my life.

"After she told us that she would be no help, she told us to do a report on our most admired person," I said.

"You can write about Daddy," my mom said.

"They have to be dead," I said. "And famous. I might pick Thomas Edison. Or Harry Houdini."

"Not Houdini!" my mom said. "That crazy magician will put ideas in your head. There will be no locking yourself in a box."

"Maybe Benjamin Franklin," I said.

"No more experiments with keys and lightning," she said.

"Don't you worry," I said. "It's the dull kind of report. All research. No action."

"Very wise of Ms. Madison," my mom said.

"Bring it along this weekend," my dad said. "You can get a lot done on the drive to Richmond."

"No, he can't," my mom said. "He'll get queasy. But it's a three-day weekend. There's plenty of quiet time in hospitals. He can work while Aunt Molly's doing her knee exercises."

"Dad said Congress made Labor Day so people could have a *rest* from working," I said. "Besides, I have a load of time before my report is due. Ten days."

"Ten days isn't as long as you think, Sport."

"It's practically half a month," I said.

"It's exactly one-third of this month," he said.

"Never fear," I said. "I've got everything under control."

The problem with my pizza-plowing system is that vegetables pile up. Luckily, my mom and dad were talking. In one

smooth move, I tipped the gross bits into my hand and dropped them under the table.

"I want to hear about Pip," my mom said.

"How do you know about Pip?"

"M.O.T.H. to M.O.T.H.," my dad said.

M.O.T.H.s are Moms On The Hill. They report to each other. Unluckily, some of them report on me.

"Mrs. Bigelow says Pip has lovely manners," my mom said.

"Mrs. Bigelow is grateful when Bart doesn't fart at funerals," my dad said.

He winked at me.

My dad and I think farts are funny. My mom says they are unmentionable and childish. Then I say I am a child and she gives my dad a look.

"Bart can fart anytime he wants," I said. "It's his major skill in life."

"Between now and the end of high school, Bart might want to get a second skill," my dad said. "I don't believe there are any jobs for a person with that talent."

"A professional farter!" I said.

I could not stop laughing.

My mom could not stop ignoring.

"Kathleen Sullivan's mom met Pip and her family at the pool. She says she is mature, quiet, and serious."

"That is the way of moms," I said.

"She was talking about Pip," my mom said.

"What's Pip like?" my dad asked.

I wrinkled my shoulders. "She's okay, I guess."

"Pip would be a good influence on you, Darling Boy," my mom said. "I mean, DB. Lucy Rose has a way of leading you and Sam straight into trouble."

My dad snorted.

"I'm serious," my mom told him. "We don't want a repeat of last year. Adam is impressionable. Lucy Rose gets ideas. He and Sam follow right along."

My dad looked at her sideways. "That's not what Mr. Pitt said, Betty."

"Mr. Pitt blames Adam for everything," my mom said.

"I like Lucy Rose," my dad said. "She's got spunk."

"We all like her," my mom said. "But it would be good for Adam to make friends with a calm person who follows rules."

I am not sure Pip is that person.

"How would you like to invite Pip to dinner when we get back from Richmond?" she asked.

"I wouldn't," I said.

Part of me would.

"New kids appreciate being included," my mom said.

"No pressure, Sport," my dad said.

"We have too many steps," I said.

"We'll picnic in the backyard," my mom said. Then she told my dad, "Pip uses a wheelchair."

I would like Pip to come over.

I would not like to be the inviter.

"Okay," I said. "She can come. If Sam can."

9

STARVED BY MY OWN MOTHER

Today our footpool met in front of Jimmy T's.

"I brought you a kiwi, Pee-wee," Sam said. "In case your mom isn't over the resolution."

"She isn't, but we took a break this weekend because we mostly ate at the hospital cafeteria," I said.

"You lucky duck!" Lucy Rose said.

"I was. Now it's back to vegetable overload," I said.

"For how long?" Jonique asked.

"My mom says it's for life," I said to her. "And she's turned against regular flour. For breakfast today she invented a chickpea-and-parsley omelet called Chomlette."

"I hope somebody else in your family gets sick soon," Sam said. "Hospital-cafeteria sick, I mean."

"I'm hoping my head off," I said.

"Was the Chomlette terrible?" Jonique said.

"I'm willing to let you taste it," I told her. "I'm carrying it with me."

"I'd rather eat a dirt sandwich," Sam said. "With ketchup they're not bad."

"Take my granola bar," Lucy Rose said. "It's a pity present. Madam made it with oatmeal and raisins."

"You can have my day-old Bubbling Brown Sugar Baby," Jonique said. "I would've gotten a fresh Peanutty Buddy but thanks to the report, I didn't have a second to go to the shop."

Jonique does homework the day she gets it.

"I was going to start on Most Admired Famous Dead Person but there's a lot to do at a hospital," I said.

"Melonhead," Lucy Rose said. "Wait a sec, do you have a pocketful of Chomlette?"

"Where else would I hide it?" I said.

"That's utterly revolting in the extreme," Lucy Rose said. "Throw it away."

"Good idea," I said. I pitched a Chomlette wad at Sam.

"In your hair, Bear!"

He threw it back.

It fell apart like confetti.

"It looks good on you, Kalamazoo!"

"I'm covered with Chomlette," Jonique said.

"We're covered," Sam said. "You have half a skink of chickpea on your shirt."

"And around fifty-five skinks in her braids," Lucy Rose said.

"Which got specially done for school," Jonique said. "Plus Lucy Rose's shorts have chickpea spots."

"I'm feeling like some got in my boots," Lucy Rose huffed.

Supersonic brain-to-brain message to Sam: Why are they acting like this is worse than the Titanic?

Message back: No idea.

"Sorry," I said.

"Ditto," Sam said.

"You should have consideration," Lucy Rose said.

They walked ahead of us for the rest of the way.

During Spanish I petted my kiwi's fur. My stomach was begging for it, but unluckily, Señora Ramirez pays equal attention to everybody.

After we said, *"Adiós, Señora,"* and she said, *"Adiós, amigos,"* Ms. Mad said, "Raise your hand if you're a polliwog."

"A what?" Amir asked.

"Polliwogs are tadpoles," Robinson said.

"I am no tadpole," Ashley said. "They're slimy."

"Sailors who have never crossed the equator are called polliwogs," Ms. Mad said.

The only hands-down person was Hannah.

"I went to Australia when I was eight months old," she said. "I was with my parents."

"Take a bow," Ms. Mad said. "You are Room Nine's only hardshell."

"Brilliant!" Hannah said.

"Some sailors celebrate crossing by getting a

tattoo of a hard-shell turtle standing on his hind legs, or King Neptune, the Roman god of the sea," Ms. Mad said.

"He's fake," Ashley said.

"He's a myth," Ms. Mad said.

I turned toward Hannah. "Did you get a tattoo?"

"No," she said.

"Good," Ms. Mad said. "I don't believe in tattooing babies."

Some people laughed.

"Do merchant marines get tattoos?" I asked.

"Some do," Ms. Mad said.

"I never had a teacher who knew so much about tattoos," I said.

"Thank you," she said.

She will probably never be interesting again. But that is news to use.

I felt like the kiwi was calling out from my pocket, "Take a bite." I gave it a pet. It was leaking.

When Ms. Mad leaned over to talk into Pip's ear, my brain said, "Take a bite." It was a demand.

I pulled up my desktop for a shield. Luckily, the kiwi was smooshed. Otherwise it would need cutting and my mom says I'm not allowed to own a Swiss Army knife until I am over thirty. I squeezed the bottom to push the top of the green seedy part up so I could bite it. I didn't expect the whole fruit to pop into my mouth. Kiwi fuzz was snagged between my teeth.

There was a hard knock on the other side of my desktop. I looked up. Ms. Mad was looking down.

"Adam," she said.

"Yerf," I said. Juice was rolling out the sides of my mouth. Furry flaps were sticking out like pointy brown tongues.

I stood up. "Ahl go ta Misser Pitt," I said.

"Sit," she said. "I don't want you spending the time you should be learning about the equator sitting in Mr. Pitt's office. We both know why you did it. You're hungry."

How could anybody call her Bad Mad?

"Fanks," I said.

I could hear Pip snickering.

"Adam, after lunch, report to the Reflecting

Table to think about your choice and the consequences."

"That won't take long at all," I said.

"It will take thirty minutes exactly," she said.

"But that's all of recess."

"Yes. If you have leftover time, use it to think about ways to improve your biography project."

So that's *why they call her Bad Mad.*

Here are the things I reflected on:

1. A great idea would be to glue mirrors to the Reflecting Table so it actually reflects.

2. What would happen if I was fishing in the Potomac River and I hooked a snakehead fish that broke the world record for largeness? And when I

reeled it in it attacked me and we had to fight on land and sea? I decided to save myself first, then the tourists who were watching.

3. I thought about Bob Born for my MAFDP. I admire him for inventing the automatic Peeps-making machine. Before 1954 the chicks had to be made one at a time, by squeezing marshmallow goo through a cake icing tube. But he's not my top most admired. Plus, Bob had help. Also, what if he isn't dead?

Recess was almost gone when Ms. Mad asked, "Do you have something you'd like to say, Adam?"

"I'm sorry for eating in the classroom, but I wasn't just plain hungry. I was starving. My mom is torturing me with health food. I'm so empty I ate the carrots and celery that were in my lunch."

Ms. Mad opened her bag and pulled out a piece of string cheese and a Baggie of mini-tomatoes.

"You have two minutes before the bell rings."

I was so shocked I blurted out, "You're not bad, Ms. Mad."

"That's nice to hear, Adam," she said.

"Due to my starvation," I said, "these actually taste okay."

"I'll tell you something the rest of the students won't know until we study nutrition in health class," she said. "Tomatoes are related to deadly nightshade, a plant that kills."

"Ha! I can't wait to tell my mom she's putting me in danger."

"Tomatoes aren't toxic. Their relatives are."

After school I caught up with Lucy Rose on the playground and told her how close we had come to being poisoned.

"Where's Jonique?" I asked.

"Going to Baking Divas to fold boxes," she said. "The Divas got an order for four hundred mini-Cuppa Coffeecakes."

"That's one lucky family," I said.

"The McBees?"

"The family getting the Cuppas."

"Where's Sam?" she asked.

"His mom's dropping him off at the library," I said. "His MAFDP is Jesse Owens."

"How did he get famous?"

"He ran so fast he won the Olympics," I said. "Do you want to walk together?"

"Okay," she said.

"I asked Pip if she wanted to come with us, but she's going to drawing class," I said.

"Am I your number four choice?" Lucy Rose asked as she pulled on her backpack straps.

It seemed like she was annoyed with me.

10

EVERYBODY HAS A DEAD PERSON EXCEPT ME

I woke up feeling great. By the time I got to the bathroom, I felt greater. On my way down the hall, I had invented a crab-style hand-walking.

Step 1: Do a handstand so your back is facing the wall but not too close.

Step 2: Bend your knees so the bottoms of your feet are on the wall.

Step 3: Walk your feet on the wall at the same time you hand-walk on the floor.

It's impossible to turn a doorknob with your feet.

I found my toothbrush in the laundry hamper. Then I remembered that tonight was the Pip dinner. My stomach went lopsided. Probably because my toothbrush tasted like used socks.

Sam and I got to Jimmy T's before Lucy Rose and Jonique.

"Do you think we should tell them about the Pip dinner?" Sam said.

"I do not," I said.

"Me either," Sam said. "Even though there's nothing the matter with it."

"They do a load of stuff without us."

"We do stuff with other people," Sam said.

"Not with girls," I said. "But Pip is more friend than girl. Right?"

"Right," Sam said. "Did your mom promise no cauliflower?"

"Yes. No cauliflower," I said. "No hidden soybeans. She's calling my Aunt Traci to get kid-friendly recipes."

"I hope it's chicken fingers," Sam said.

"It could be," I told him. "Aunt Traci is so kid-friendly my cousin gets to have a TV in his room."

"Seriously?" Sam said. "My mom says I can have a TV in my room when I'm married."

"Which means never," I said.

"That's why she says it," Sam said.

"My mom says it's uncivilized," I told Sam. "I said so am I. But she said I'm a work in progress."

"Whatever that means," Sam said.

"We'll probably still have salad at dinner," I said.

"I like salad," Sam said.

Once we got settled in Room Nine, Ms. Mad told us, "Line up. We're going to quietly walk down the hall to the library. Mrs. Ochmanek will show you how to research your most admired person."

She wheeled Pip to the front of the line.

"I can do it myself," Pip told her.

Ms. Mad jumped back like the handles were hot.

"Of course you can," she said.

Sam whispered to Jonique, "Who's your Most Admired Famous Dead Person?"

"Sojourner Truth," Jonique said. "Only when she was born her name was Isabella. She changed it when she started giving speeches about women being equal to men and slaves deserving freedom."

"I was going to write about Sarah Bernhardt," Lucy Rose said. "On account of she was so excellent-O that the public called her the Divine Sarah and the Most Famous Actress the World Has Ever Known. People paid lots to see her shows at the Moulin Rouge theater, which is fancy like you can't believe and is in France, which is a country that is exotic in the extreme."

"You know all that about her and she's not your MAFDP?" I said. "What a waste."

"I decided she couldn't have been that great. If she was, she would have been the star of some ultra-terrific shows like My Fair Lady or Grease or Anything Goes. You can't be the best if you don't know how to tap dance."

"I know that's right," Jonique said.

"So I picked the deluxe, delightful, talented-like-you-can't-believe, utterly famous Broadway actress Miss Ethel Merman."

"I never heard of her," Sam said.

"Well, you should have," Lucy Rose told him. "According to Pop she was filled to her gills with razzmatazz."

"I don't know what razzmatazz is," I said.

"Yes, you do, because you know me and I'm filled to my gills with it," she said. "I have the razzmatazz personality. My report is going to have a live-action part. It's me singing 'There's No Business Like Show Business' like no business I know."

"That's a load of businesses," I said.

"Lucy Rose," Ms. Mad said. "No singing while researching."

"How did she know it was me?" Lucy Rose whispered.

"You guys are ahead of me," I whispered. "I'm still looking for an admirable person."

Lucy Rose made pop eyes at me. "You don't have one?"

"You'd best pick a person," Jonique said.

"Good googa-mooga," I said. "You're acting like it's due tomorrow. I have time."

"Write about Fred Astaire, the dancingest man of all time," Lucy Rose said. "He had so many moves he could dance with a broom."

"I am not doing a dancing man," I said.

At recess, Sam, Pip, and I threw rocks at the kickball that's been stuck in the maple tree since last year. Pip has great aim.

Lucy Rose and Jonique tied their ankles together with Lucy Rose's yellow bandana.

"We're practicing three-legged racing," Jonique yelled. "Time us."

"Ready, steady, GO!" I shouted.

"Pip," Sam said. "Are you coming to Melonhead's with us after school?"

"I have physical therapy until five-fifteen," she said.

"How come you go to therapy?" I asked.

"They exercise my legs," she said.

"So you'll be able to walk?" I said.

"Nope," she said.

"Time, please?" Lucy Rose hollered.

"I lost track," I shouted. "Sorry."

She stomped down the hill, which made one of Jonique's feet stomp too. Her other foot had to run to keep up.

Lucy Rose's face was so pink you couldn't see her freckles. "For heaven's to pity's sake, Melonhead," she yelled. "This is serious. We could have just broken the world record for three-legged racing, but now we will never know. You should have regret galore."

"We do," Sam said. "But cheer up. You weren't that fast."

"We were talking to Pip and forgot about you guys," I explained.

When we were going back inside, Pip said, "My sister will drop me off after P.T."

"Drop you where?" Lucy Rose asked.

"At the library," I lied.

"On my head," Pip said a split nanosecond later. She's a speedy thinker.

I could tell Lucy Rose didn't believe the head-dropping part. She might not have believed the library part. But if I hadn't lied she might want to come. My mom would say no, due to me being impressionable. Also, I would sort of rather it just be Pip, Sam, and me.

11

PIP COMES OVER

Sam had a grand-slam idea. "Let's pour sugar down ant holes."

I improved it.

"Fruit by the Foot!" I said.

"Ant Town in your own front yard!" Sam said.

"We'll give them sidewalks."

He high-fived me. "Brainiac attack, Mac!"

"Ditto, Kiddo," I said.

I got two yards of Fruit feet.

"We're lucky I found it," I said. "My mom has decided Fruit doesn't count as fruit."

"Blue for the ants. Red for me. Green for you," Sam said.

My mom came out to see if Pip was there yet.

"No, but would you like to see our sixty-seven-million-dollar smiles?" I said.

"Why did you do that, DB?" she asked.

"To impress Pip," Sam said.

"Red and green teeth will make an impression," my mom said. "And if you keep covering your teeth with sugar, you'll be able to dazzle her with dentures."

"Thank you," I said. "We want her to think we're hilarious."

I don't know why I felt nervous.

We were watching the ants march across our suspended bridge made of Fruit when Pip's minivan stopped in front of our house. The side door opened and a metal square slid out automatically. When Pip rolled on it, the square lowered and she wheeled onto the sidewalk.

The first thing she said was "Fantastic teeth."

"Fantastic car elevator," I said.

"You want to do your teeth?" I asked.

"I can dust the ants off," Sam said.

"No, thanks," she said.

"Who makes your car lifter go up and down?" Sam asked.

"I do," Pip said.

"Later, Pip!" her sister screamed out the window.

"She's fast," Sam said.

"Maude wants to get to Trader Joe's before the after-work rush," Pip said.

"Man-o-man. She is made of luck," I said. "I would go crazy from happiness if I could pick our food."

"The day Maude got her driver's permit, my mom gave her the car keys and said, 'I'm retiring.' She told my dad keeping five kids in food is a full-time job."

"I wish my parents had five kids," I said. "All boys. No offense."

"Ditto," Sam said. "Except I'd keep Julia."

"What happens when Maude goes to college?" I asked.

"It will be Millicent's turn," Pip said. "I hope she is done being a vegetarian by then."

"That is a thing I will *never* be," I said.

My mom came outside.

"Welcome, Pip," she said. "I've heard such nice things about you."

"You have?" Pip said.

"Mr. Melon is still at work," my mom said. "But don't worry about the stairs, Pip. We'll eat in the back garden."

"Mom, would you ever let me do our grocery shopping?"

She laughed so hard her eyeballs shined.

"You are one funny kid, Adam Melon," she said. "Dinner will be ready in half an hour."

We hung around on the sidewalk.

"Is your mom a good cook?" Pip asked.

"She is an excellent eater," I said. "Restaurants must love her. She orders the things nobody else wants. Like trout and liver. Luckily, at home she's more of a chicken fingers lady."

"She makes delicious noodles with butter," Sam said.

"I love both those things," Pip said.

I skipped over the Great Cauliflower Mistake.

"Do you like our class?" Sam asked.

"Most of the kids are good to great," she said. "Ashley is a bully."

"How about Ms. Mad?" I asked.

"I heard she was Godzilla, so she's better than I expected. But she's a Hovercraft."

"What's that?" Sam asked.

"A teacher who stands over my head a lot," Pip said. "An over-helper."

"She does?" I said.

"Because she doesn't hover over you," Pip said. "Remember when I talked to you and Ashley tattled? Ms. Mad blamed you. I got off free. Hovercraft teachers think I'm fragile. But I've normalized the others. I just have to figure out what will work on Ms. Mad."

"I'd love it if I got off free," I said.

"You wouldn't if Ms. Mad went gooshy on you. She told me I can talk to Mr. Pitt anytime I want to."

"I can soak my head in a bucket of boogers anytime I want to," I said. "But why would I want to?"

I am a comical genius.

"That's what I said," Pip told me. "Not the booger part. The why-would-I-want-to part. But Ms. Mad said that someday I might and that he is understanding."

"Don't believe her," I said. "He's the opposite. He always says, 'I *cannot* understand why you would do this.'"

"Do what?" Pip asked.

"Anything," Sam said. "Like when we brought Gumbo to meet Mr. Johnson, the custodian, and the dog got away and ran across the gym and stole the lunch lady's lunch."

"What did Mr. Pitt do?" Pip asked.

"He said, 'This should not have happened,'" I said in my Pitt voice.

"Melonhead said, 'She's a dog, Mr. Pitt. That's what dogs do,'" Sam told her.

"Mr. Pitt blamed me for taking off her collar," I said. "Which was an accident. We were loosening it in case it was choking her. He doesn't care about poodles."

"I do not call that understanding," Sam said.

"It's not," Pip said. "Now, I want to see the inside of your house."

12.

DISAPPEARING PANTS WOULD BE LESS EMBARRASSING THAN THIS DINNER

I was nervous about pushing Pip up the stairs because what if I tipped the chair too far back and she flipped over? Then I figured it out.

"You're as skinny as wire," I said. "Sam and I will carry you. Then we'll bring up your wheelchair. E-Z P-Z."

"I'm not skinny," she said. "And you won't carry me."

Pip used the secret-compartment arms to boost herself out of the chair. Then she grabbed the railing and lowered herself onto the second-to-bottom step.

"Can I try to do that?" I asked.

"Sure," she said.

I sat in Pip's chair and tried to lift myself with no leg power.

"Your arms look like chicken wings," Sam said.

I could feel my face broiling. "It's a bad angle for me," I said.

"Push up, Pup," Sam said.

"It's harder than you think, Linc," I said.

Pip laughed. "Go ahead, Ted. Do it."

Rhyming is between Sam and me. Usually I don't like people to horn in. This time it didn't bug me.

I was glad that Sam couldn't push himself up either.

Pip used her arms to lift herself up to the next step.

"Ah, you go up backward," I said.

"Buttward," she said.

I hooted. Sam laughed so hard he had to wipe his nose on his T-shirt.

We carried Pip's chair up to the porch. It was heavier than you'd think.

"Park it next to the railing," she said. "And put the brake on."

She grabbed the rail, pulled herself up, and plopped back into her seat.

Sam held our front door open. Pip rolled herself into our vestibule.

"We have to leave our shoes out here," I said. "My mom thinks they bring filth into the house."

"Not mine," Pip said.

That was when I realized why her shoes always look new.

I gave a tour of the living room that kids aren't allowed in.

"Who wants to arm wrestle me?" Pip asked.

You have to do what your guest wants. "To the dining room," I said.

"I'll try," Sam said.

"You'll die," Pip told him.

After she beat Sam two out of two, I took a turn.

I lost one match and was about to lose the second when my mom came through the kitchen door.

"Adam! What are you doing? This is no way to treat a girl." She was screeching.

"That's what I told him," Pip said. "But he made me do it anyway."

I could not speak. My mom could. "Adam Melon, I am appalled."

Pip burst out laughing.

"Kidding!" she said. "It was my idea and I won."

"My goodness," my mom said.

Then she realized something. "Pip, you're upstairs. Don't tell me you let the boys carry you."

"I would never," Pip said. "They're not strong enough. Melonhead gets distracted. And they both drop stuff."

My mom exhaled. Her yoga teacher says that's nerve-calming. It doesn't work.

"We could have carried you no problem," Sam said to Pip.

"The other day I lifted my mom and she's like three of you," I said.

"Since you all are inside now, we may as well eat here," my mom said.

"I'll set the table, Mrs. Melon," Pip said.

"Thanks, Pip," she said. "I'll take care of it. You all wash your hands before dinner."

"Sam's and mine got clean when we were making the ants' swimming pool, Mom."

"Both sides. Use soap," my mom said.

"How come you have a sink in the hall?" Pip asked.

"It's from over a century ago, when our house was built. Back then flowers got water from their own sinks. It makes zero sense."

"I like it," Pip said. "No skinny doorway."

Then Pip said one of the smartest things I have ever heard. "You only eat with one hand. Washing the leftover one is a complete waste."

"Genius times infinity," I said, and I thought up an instant time-and-water saver. "Sam washes my hand. I wash yours, and you wash Sam's. All at once. Three hands in three seconds."

Why did I say that? She'll think I'm trying to hold her hand.

Pip grabbed the soap and said, "Hands in the sink."

When we were done I compared my right and left.

"It worked," I said. "My left hand is still gray."

"Cool," Sam said.

"Funny," Pip said.

I'm the type who would rather be funny than cool.

I moved a chair so Pip could have the best side of the table. Sam and I sat on the side with the valuable painting. My mom calls the scrolly gold frame ro-co-co. Aunt Traci says that means overdone.

"Ready?" My mom came through the swinging door like a movie waitress.

"The first plate goes to Pip," she said.

I could not believe what I was seeing.

Please be joking.

"Princess Pip, your dinner is served."

"My dinner is a horse's head?" Pip asked.

"A unicorn head," my mom said. "My sister tells me girls love unicorns."

Decapitated unicorns?

"My sister Mavis is saving up to buy a real one," Pip said. "She's six."

"It's not only beautiful. It's healthy," my mom said. "The unicorn's mane is cabbage slaw. The horn is an ice cream cone frosted with pink mayonnaise."

"How did it get pink?" Pip asked.

"Beet juice," my mom said. "Isn't that smart?"

"Wow," Pip said.

"That idea came from my own head," my mom said. "Once I got going I discovered I have a wide creative streak."

"I can tell," Pip said.

"The horn is filled with pureed yellow wax beans."

"What's the face made of?" Pip asked.

My mom turned her plate so the unicorn's nose pointed away from Pip. "Now you see an ordinary butternut squash," my mom said.

She re-turned it. "But before your eyes, the squash is transformed into a unicorn head. The eyelashes are dill weed. This unicorn is chock-full of potassium."

Supersonic message to Sam: She is making Pip eat weeds.

"Isn't it terrific?"

"Terrific," Pip said.

"Adam's Aunt Traci drove down from Baltimore this morning to bring me a cookbook called *Vegalicious! Making Food Fun!*"

"By making it look like a unicorn?" Pip said.

"The author, Bernice Bombono, says children reject vegetables because parents don't present them in exciting ways. Those dull days are over."

I couldn't look at Pip.

"The head is filled with Bombono's Magic Mix," my mom said. "It's really yogurt with spinach, blue cheese, and bean sprouts."

"Trick food must take a long time to make," Pip said.

"About four hours," my mom told her. "There's lots of chopping. But it's worth it. Bernice Bombono says, 'A child's best friends should be Nutritious and Delicious.'"

She pointed at Sam. "You're next."

She was back in a flash.

"What is it?" Sam asked.

"A veggie-powered sports car, of course," she said. "Doesn't it look real?"

"Real?" Sam asked.

My face was burning.

Sam was in shock.

Pip looked dizzy.

"The main part of the car is a hollowed-out baby zucchini," my mom said. "The hood really works."

Sam peeled back a green flap of zucchini skin.

"Take a guess what's under the motor," my mom said.

"Bombono's Magic Mix," Sam said.

"Bingo! The engine parts are turkey strips, grapes, hard-boiled eggs, and sunflower seeds. I made the hoses out of radish peelings. The knobs are corn kernels. It's all held together with home-made barbecue mayonnaise."

"That's some engine," I said.

"No one would guess it's food," Pip said.

"Look at the steering wheel. It's a carrot coin with a raisin horn. The seats are mushroom caps. Can you believe the wheels are brussels sprouts?" my mom said. "Adam, I'll be back with yours."

When the kitchen door swung shut, Pip whispered, "No matter how you disguise them, brussels sprouts are still small, stinky cabbages."

I whispered back, "I'm sorry for inviting you!"

"I'm sorry to be invited," Pip said.

"Ditto," Sam said. "Even Julia wouldn't eat this. And she eats Milk-Bones."

"Ta-dah!" my mom said. "Captain Adam, here's your yacht."

I'd rather have a dinghy.

"The hull is half a Japanese eggplant cut the long way and baked. Aunt Traci says the beauty of eggplant is that it absorbs the taste of whatever is nearby."

It smelled like sock.

"The deck is made of turkey planks. The galley is underneath."

"Is it loaded with Bombono Magic Mix?" I asked.

"Good guess, DB."

"What's DB?" Pip asked.

"Darling Boy," my mom said. "He doesn't want people to know I call him that, so we use initials."

Pip is people, Mom.

13

MELONHEAD, BOY GENIUS

When I looked at my yacht, all I could think was *Oh, my ruined taste buds.* Also that Aunt Traci is a failure of a relative.

My next thought was worse: *When food takes a load of work to make, you have to eat it.*

"What's in the yellow bowl?" Sam asked.

"Crab salad," my mom said. "It's protein-packed and delicious."

She scooped a pile onto her plate and sat down.

"I'm stuffed," Sam said.

"Sam," my mom laughed. "Twenty minutes ago, you said you were so hungry your belly button was scraping against your spine."

I kicked Sam's shin under the table.

"He's kidding, Mom," I said.

Supersonic message: This is a no-choice situation.

I took a bite the size of my eyeball. Mistake.

"Well?" my mom said.

"Mmm," I said.

"Tasty-ola," Sam said.

"Creative," Pip said.

My mom smiled. "Once again, my sister was right," she said. "I worried you kids might be too sophisticated for these recipes. But the book says for kids age three to one hundred."

Sam's mouth was packed to the gums with many car parts. His cheeks were lumpy.

Pip cut her unicorn into mini-chunks. Then she cut the chunks in half. I think her plan was to keep cutting until the pieces were sand-size.

Then, for the second time in a week, we were saved by the phone.

"I'm sorry to be rude but it must be Adam's dad calling from the office," my mom said. "I'll be quick."

The instant the door shut, Sam spit two wads of car into his hands. "It tastes like slime," he said. "I can't eat it."

"You want slime? Try unicorn brains," Pip said.

"I'll throw up if I eat crabmeat," Sam said.

"Honey," my mom was saying, "I feel like Supermom. I mean, yes, it was complicated but you should have seen their faces when they saw their dinners. They couldn't believe I made them."

Then she laughed. "You're right," my mom said. "Pip probably never gets unicorn at home."

"That's true," Pip said.

She scrubbed her tongue with her napkin. "Sorry," she said. "I had to scrape off the aftertaste."

"Quick!" I said. "We're dumping this stuff out the window."

Pip put her plate in her lap, backed up, and spun around.

"It won't open," Sam whispered.

"Push the top up," Pip said. "I'll pull the bottom."

"I'll do it," I said.

"No time," she said. "I'm stronger."

We could hear my mom telling my dad, "I should get back to the table so I can wallow in my success."

"Oh, my sweet orangutan! She's about to hang up," I said.

That was when I got the idea of the century.

"Escape hatch!" I whispered.

I flopped to my knees and poked my fingers through the golden vent cover on the floor and yanked.

"Hurry!" Sam hissed.

My mom's voice came through the air. "I miss you more."

Pip looked down at the blackness. "Where does it go?"

"Down the heat duct and into the furnace," I said. "Where it will burn up."

"In the summer?" Sam asked.

"E-Z P-Z. I'll turn the heat on and BAM! The evidence is ashes."

Pip tipped her plate and said, "Goodbye, little unicorn head."

Sam chucked in his car.

I whispered, "So long, yacht."

"Grab the crab," Pip said.

A flash and a half later we were back at the table. It was the closest call of my life. My whole head was pouring sweat.

My mom looked at me with Ping-Pong-ball eyes.

She knows!

"I'm sorry, Mom," I said.

"Sorry? I'm thrilled. *You cleaned your plates!* Don't be sorry."

"We're sorry we finished without you," Pip said.

"We couldn't stop ourselves," Sam said.

True.

"You ate the crab salad?" she said.

"We cleaned out that bowl," Pip told her.

Also true.

"I never expected that you'd eat crabmeat," my mom said.

"You didn't?" Sam asked.

"No," she said. "I considered it grown-up food. Now that I know you like it, it's worth the money."

I saw Sam out of the sides of my eyes. His lips wiggle when he's nervous.

"DB, I am sorry I didn't learn to cook this way years ago. You might be six inches taller today," my mom said.

"I like my height," I said.

While Pip and Sam brought the unbreakables into the kitchen, I sponged the table and checked the vent. Nothing but black. Right now my MAFDP is the one who invented furnaces.

After dinner we sat on the porch and ate Smart Blondies.

"They're from Baking Divas," my mom told Pip. "I've given up baking since I put spinach in the brownies. That was a crazy idea."

Crazy like a unicorn.

After my mom went inside, Pip said, "That was the weirdest dinner I ever ate."

"Didn't eat," Sam said.

"But I had a great time. I can't wait to tell Millicent about my unicorn."

Stomach tilt! *Everybody on Capitol Hill will know by morning. An M.O.T.H. will call.*

"Don't worry. She'll keep it in the Cone of Silence," Pip said. "I don't like people blabbing about my family."

"Are they strange?" Sam asked.

"My dad calls us the Eccentrics," she said. "My mom sings in front of my friends."

"Your mom's a singer?" I asked.

"A bad one," Pip said.

My dad got home before Sam and Pip got picked up.

"Way to chow down on vegetables, kids," he said. "Thanks to a mighty creative chef."

"Thank you," my mom said. "I feel like an artiste."

"You worked hard," Sam said.

"Thank you, Sam," my mom said. "I'm so pleased that you loved your sports car."

Pip went down the steps the same way she went up, only forward. My dad carried her chair down.

Mr. Alswang walked over. He was pushing an

empty stroller. Baby Julia was crawling beside him. She barked at Pip.

"My littlest sister Merrie was a dog last year," Pip said.

"How long did it last?" Sam asked.

"Weeks," Pip said. "She still growls at birds. Oh, Maude's here. Thanks for inviting me, Mrs. Melon. Next time Melonhead and Sam can eat at my house."

Maude beeped the horn. "See you tomorrow, guys," Pip said. She gave Julia a head pat. "See you later, dog."

"We'll pick you up on the way to school," I said.

After they left, I sat on the top step and listened to my parents talk about Congressman Buddy Boyd's dream of getting oranges made the national fruit.

"The apple growers won't go for that," my mom said.

"Not a chance," my dad said.

"Good night, Parents," I yelled. "I'm going to sleep now."

"How's the biography coming?" my dad said.

"It's coming," I said.

"Planning ahead makes things easy, doesn't it?" he said.

"Sweet dreams, DB."

I felt bad about wasting her work. Also for being slippery about my project. I almost said my mom could go back to calling me Darling Boy.

Guilt made me brush my teeth nonstop for fifty seconds and take a shower. I didn't use soap. It smells ladyish. Then I put on my glow-in-the-dark constellation T-shirt, turned out the light in my room, and listened for footsteps.

They didn't come until ten-fifteen. It took twenty more minutes for the light coming from the crack under my parents' bedroom door to disappear. To prevent step creaking, I slid down the banister. Since it was dark, I didn't know I was near the newel post until my butt smashed into it. I wish our post was round like Madam and Pop's. Corners stab.

I crept like a ninja.

First stop: living room.

Turn the furnace thermostat dial to ninety.

Done.

To the kitchen.

Grab a loaf of raisin bread.

Crawl back to my room on my elbows, like a soldier, dragging my bruised butt.

Luckily, my survival jar of lingonberry jelly was under my bed. I made an instant sheet tent held up by my head. Three double-decker jam sandwiches revived my brain.

At midnight, I went back down and turned off the heat.

I am lucky to live in a house with a built-in evidence destroyer.

14
A BLOODY MESS

Once I saw a lady on TV who said that in emergencies your brain takes over and tells you what to do.

It's true.

When I woke up this morning I was lying on a dark, damp pool. My sheets were streaked with red.

BLOOD! I rolled over on my fork! I bet my lungs are pierced. I'm going to deflate. Breathe lightly. No pain. I'm freezing. That means I'm in shock. My body is numb. I bled so much I doubt I have enough energy left to crawl to the door. Roll over gently.

My face landed on the bigger side of the dark sticky spot. As I opened my mouth to scream, "Call 911," I accidently licked my sheet.

When you think you are dying and you find out you're just sleeping in a load of lingonberry jelly, you get up happy.

I shoved my sheets in the hamper and dumped dirty clothes on top.

I charged through the kitchen door like a water buffalo.

"Good morning, Mommo!" I yelled. "Hello, Daddy-O."

"Good morning, DB. Go back upstairs and take off yesterday's shirt."

"Be fair, Mom," I said. "It's my only Washington Nationals shirt. I've worn dirtier clothes to school."

"Adam, I'm not in the mood to debate this. Daddy and I barely slept."

"I'm not the one who told you to stay awake," I said.

"Of course not," she said. "We were roasting half the night. Then we froze. Now I'm exhausted."

I didn't know what to say, so I stood there.

"New day. New shirt. New Melon Family Guideline for Life," my dad said.

I loaded my cargo pockets with Golden Grahams and Frosted Flakes.

"Why are there green spots in the eggs?" I asked.

"They're scallions," my mom said. "They give the eggs a certain zing."

I don't want zing.

"I'll eat a frozen waffle while I walk," I said. "The cold will keep me from fainting from the heat."

"Sit down, Darling Boy."

"I can't. If you're late, you get the Reflecting Table. Believe me, it doesn't matter if you were hit by a dump truck and carried off by vultures who drop you in the sewers. If you're late, you reflect."

"What can you do to avoid that?"

"I'm glad you asked, Dad," I said. "If I'm late, I'll make a U-turn and come back home. You don't have to reflect for being absent."

"No," my dad said. "If we're wrong, we admit. If we're late, we reflect. It's the Code of the Melons."

"Gotta go. The footpool is waiting at Jimmy T's."

When Jonique saw me she yelled, "Step on it."

She thinks being tardy is a crime. "Turn at the corner. We're picking up Pip," I said.

"Pip's coming with us?" Lucy Rose asked.

"Melonhead invited her," Sam said.

I gave him the look of double death.

Supersonic message to Sam: DO NOT say Pip came over for dinner.

"Her house is on the way," I said.

"Is Pip going to come with us every day?" Jonique asked.

"Maybe," I said.

"We're used to the way it is," Lucy Rose said.

"You like Pip," I said.

"I go for funny people," Lucy Rose said. "But she shouldn't come with us every day on account it's like we are a club of four."

"Nobody told me we were a club," I said.

"I said it's *like* we are."

"She might slow us down, and then we'll be late," Jonique said.

"You guys can peel off. Sam and I will get Pip," I said.

"We'll go," Lucy Rose said. "But you should have asked us before you told her."

Pip was so speedy she got to school a half block ahead of us.

"I am the alpha dog," she said. Then she played air guitar and sang "Leader of the Pack."

We made it to lineup a split hair of a second after it started moving.

Ms. Madison was at the door. "Talking should stop when one foot is inside the school," she said.

"Which foot?" I yelled. "Left or right?"

She didn't answer.

15

PIP TO THE RESCUE

*T*he first thing Ms. Mad said after morning announcements was "Be seated, cartographers."

Supersonic message to Sam: I don't know what that means, but it's bad.

"You may prefer to be called mapmakers," she said.

Cancel supersonic message.

"Ethan," Ms. Mad said. "Please pass out the markers. Marisol will give each student one piece of drawing paper. We are going to be making maps of the thirteen countries that are on the equator."

I'm in favor of mapmaking.

"We will be working in pairs," she said. "Raise your hand if you would like to draw the map for Ecuador."

She picked Robinson Gold and Kathleen Sullivan.

Ashley wanted Indonesia for a map and Marisol for a partner.

"Yes on Indonesia," Ms. Mad told her. "The other member of your team will be Bart Bigelow."

Ashley acted like her head had been dipped in poison. "P-U," she said.

"That's inappropriate, Ashley," Ms. Mad said. "Recess at the Reflecting Table."

Alexandra and I got Brazil. Sam and Marisol had to draw Kenya.

"Next up: Republic of the Congo," Ms. Mad said.

Ashley waved her hand like a windmill.

"Do you have something to add, Ashley?" Ms. Mad asked.

"Yes," she said.

"This is on topic?" Ms. Mad asked.

"It's a safety report," Ashley said.

"We always have time for safety," Ms. Mad said.

"Melonhead's balancing on two chair legs. Again."

That shocked me so much I tipped backward. Luckily, my head landed on Hannah's desktop. Even upside down Hannah's face looked annoyed.

"That is tattling, Ashley," Ms. Mad said. "And, Adam, that is a safety issue. What are we going to do about that?"

Hello, Mr. Pitt. Goodbye, sweet freedom.

"Excuse me, Ms. Madison," Pip called out. "I have a problem."

Ms. Mad stopped glaring at me.

"Yes, Pip?" she said.

"My red marker is dried out."

"I'll get you a fresh one from the supply closet," Ms. Mad said.

I tore a page out of my new composition book and wrote a note to Sam. "Pip saved me. At her own personal risk." I dropped it on the floor and gave it a flick with my high-top. It landed by Lucy Rose.

Safe.

It came back fast.

Inside was Lucy Rose's handwriting. "For heaven's to Pete's sake, Melonhead, Pip didn't know she was saving you. She accidently saved you because her marker ran out. There was zero risk."

"Stealing mail is a crime," I whispered.

"Real mail," she hissed. "Notes don't count."

16

THE CHAMPIONSHIP

"Of all the people in the world, who is the one you would most like to talk to?" Ms. Mad asked the class after we finished our maps.

"Is this about the MAFDP?" I asked.

"Most Admired Famous Dead People," Sam said.

"This is about live people," she said. "They don't have to be famous, but it must be someone you feel passionate about."

Everybody laughed. Bart made smooching noises and stamped his sneakers on the floor.

"That is not what I meant, Bartholomew," Ms. Mad said.

"*Passionate* means the feeling is intense. It can describe love, or anger, or devotion," Ms. Mad said. "Robinson, you're a passionate soccer fan. Would you like to interview a champion goalie?"

"I would love it," she said.

"We get to meet anybody we want?" Amir asked.

"Each of you is going to email a letter to someone you feel passionate about. Tell that person about yourself. Ask questions," she said. "And hope they write back."

"I don't know any fashion designer addresses," Pierra said.

"Mrs. Ochmanek will help with that," she said. "Now the job is to think."

Here's what I was thinking: *Two more hours until lunch.*

The hungrier I got, the less I could think about the letter. Then it was like my stomach spoke to me. There is one person I am passionate about.

Dear Ms. Bombono,
    You are starving children. My aunt gave

your recipes to my mom. Please do not write any more books.

> Sincerely,
> Adam Melon aka Melonhead

At recess Ms. Madison said, "It's sweltering outside. Grab a shady spot under the chestnut tree, Pip."

"May I take my Capri Sun?" Pip asked.

"It's against the rules to eat or drink on the playground, Ms. Madison," Ashley said.

"I am a teacher, Ashley," Ms. Mad said. "I can choose to make an exception to the rule."

"Nobody else gets to drink outside," Ashley said.

"That's enough, Ashley," Ms. Mad said.

Lucy Rose stood in front of her with her hands on her hips. "Ashley, it's not the easiest to be the new kid. I know from personal experiences."

"Go away, bug," Ashley said.

She knew Ms. Mad was too far away to hear.

"It must be nice to have a teacher for your personal servant, Pip," she said.

Pip sucked her Capri Sun until the foil pouch collapsed.

Then she locked her eyeballs on Ashley's eyeballs and said, "What's your problem?"

"I'm allergic to teachers' pets," she said.

"Me too," Pip said.

"You're allergic to yourself?" Ashley said.

I had a brainflash.

I bent down and acted like I was tying my shoe and whispered, "Challenge her, Pip."

Pip went for it.

"Hey, Ashley. I'll make you a bet."

"What do I win?"

"If you win, I'll be your personal servant for a week, and if I win, you'll be my personal servant," Pip said.

"What's the contest?" Ashley asked.

"Arm wrestling."

"I'll beat you in two seconds," Ashley told her.

"Maybe," Pip said.

"Hope you enjoy being my servant," Ashley said.

The whole fifth grade followed them to the picnic table. Ashley sat on the bench. Pip pulled up at the end, opened her secret compartment, and took out an orange glove with no fingers.

"That's cheating," Ashley said.

"No, it's not," Pip said. "It's to keep our hands from sliding on each other's sweat."

"I'll be the ref," I said. "Ready?"

They nodded.

"Go!"

Sam and I were the only calm ones. Nobody else knew the Power of Pip.

"Ashley's elbow is off the table!" Kathleen screamed.

"Against the rules," Bart Bigelow shouted.

"The wood is hurting my skin," Ashley said.

"No excuses!" Lucy Rose said.

Pip pushed one way. Ashley pushed the other.

"Halfway down," Sam said.

"Whole way down," I yelled.

The crowd went nuts.

Pip smiled and handed Ashley her Capri Sun trash and said, "Servant, please put this in the recycle bin."

"Anybody could win if they had a glove," Ashley said.

"Get one," Pip told her. "I'll have a rematch anytime."

Ashley stinks at losing.

On the way home from school, Lucy Rose said, "Is Pip walking with us tomorrow morning? I don't care personally but Jonique is a timely person."

"Pip didn't make us late," I said.

"Not today," Lucy Rose said. "But she could."

"Anybody could," I said.

17

THE POP REPORT

After school, Lucy Rose, Jonique, Sam, and I stopped off at Madam and Pop's.

"Madam made frozen grapes," Pop said. "She claims they are delicious."

He filled up a big red bowl.

"I never heard grapes rattle before," Sam said.

"If vegetables tasted like these I'd eat a snootful," I said.

"Madam enjoys making multipurpose food," Pop said.

"So does Melonhead's mom," Jonique said.

"Tell him," Lucy Rose said. "It will make you laugh your lips off, Pop."

"It was a tragedy to us," Sam said.

We sat on the morning room sofa. Pop sat in his brown chair on the other side of the old trunk that probably was built by pirates.

Usually Lucy Rose is overly dramatic. But even though she hadn't been there, she was telling this story right. Pop's eyeballs kept growing. It wasn't the whole story. When Sam and I told Lucy Rose and Jonique, we'd skipped over Pip and the unicorn. Also the part about burning dinner in the furnace.

When Lucy Rose was done, Pop said, "That's a love story."

My ears burned. "Definitely *not*," I said.

"Sure it is," Pop said. "I wish I'd seen these works of art. They must have been stupendous."

"If stupendous means crazy," Sam said.

"It means you're stunned and astonished to your bones," Lucy Rose said. "Which anybody would be. Especially me."

"Your head would have flipped off your neck if you had seen Pip's unicorn," I said.

Lucy Rose's mouth flopped open. Her face looked sunburned.

My stomach felt like I swallowed a real yacht that was sinking.

"Pip was at your house? For the vehicle dinner?" she asked.

I wanted to kick my own butt.

"You've never invited me over for supper," Lucy Rose said. "Or Jonique."

"But I've eaten at Madam and Pop's a jillion times," I said. "So has Jonique."

"Not the same," she said.

"We sat with the Melons at the end-of-year picnic," Jonique said.

"Also not the same," Lucy Rose said.

"Be happy you were left out," Sam said. "We said it was the worst dinner we ever saw."

"Melonhead, you picked Pip over me and Jonique."

"Pip was my mom's idea," I said.

"You could've invited us, too," she said.

"I couldn't. My mom thinks you inspire me to get in trouble."

"Ha!" Lucy Rose said. "Your mom blames me? That's rich. Not rich like wealthy. Rich like completely not likely to happen in this lifetime."

"I know," I said.

"Did you defend me to your mother?" she asked.

"My dad said you have spunk," I said.

"But what did *you* say?"

"Nothing," I said. "But I should have."

She stomped out of the morning room and up the stairs. Jonique ran after her.

"I'm a hundred percent sorry!" I yelled. "I'll tell my mom you don't lead me. I'll ask if you can come over for dinner."

She didn't answer. When I looked up the steps, Madam was hugging Lucy Rose. Jonique was patting her back. It sounded like she was crying.

"Pop," I said. "Lucy Rose is so mad she might not be my friend anymore. Tell me how to fix this."

"That's something worth thinking about," Pop said.

What kind of answer is that?

18

A BAD SPOT

"Mom, I'm home!"

"Don't yell, Adam," she said. "I'm in the dining room setting the table."

"Is Lucy Rose coming for dinner?"

"No," my mom said. "Why?"

"I invited her," I said.

She kissed my forehead. "DB, I'm flattered that you want to invite your friends over to eat my creations, but I can't whip up unicorns at the drop of a spoon."

"No more unicorns!" I said.

"What?"

"I mean yes, more unicorns. Lucy Rose wants to see your creations."

She put her hand on my shoulder. "Something's wrong," she said. "A mother knows, DB. Nothing is ever so bad that you can't tell me."

"Lucy Rose found out that Pip got invited here."

"Oh, dear," my mom said. "Her feelings are hurt. She is thinking, 'Mrs. Melon never made me a fabulous unicorn.'"

She's probably leaving the unicorn out of her thoughts.

"Mom, Lucy Rose is no trouble starter. I should have told you. She doesn't get me in situations. Sam and I get each other in them. By accident. That's why she got upset when I told her what you said about her bad influence."

"You told her?" my mom squealed.

"We're friends. We tell each other things. Only not anymore. She gave up talking to me."

"Why would you tell her something that would hurt her feelings?"

"How was I supposed to know that?" I asked. "I don't mind when Sam's parents say it's my fault that he got in trouble."

"Sam's parents say that?" she asked.

"Sometimes they blame Sam for getting me in trouble. Usually they say we got each other into it. It doesn't hurt our feelings."

"I should not have said that about Lucy Rose," she said. "I feel dreadful."

"You should," I told her.

"Darling Boy."

"DB," I said.

"What we talk about in our family stays in our family," my mom said.

"Nobody ever told me we have a Cone of Silence," I said.

"That's exactly what we have," she said. "Good way to put it. I'm going to write it on the Guidelines for Life poster. Wait, that won't work. People will read it and think we talk about them."

"Mom," I said, "you are a lady. How do I get Lucy Rose to like me again?"

"Write her a note," my mom said. "Tell her how you feel."

"That works?"

"I hope so," my mom said. "I'm writing my own apology."

"I never saw her this mad," I said.

"Write the note. Then get back to your report. But first, tell me if you smell something."

"Good or bad?" I asked.

"Bad," she said.

"Nope," I said.

"Take your shower early to-day," she said. "Something smells and I'm afraid it's you."

I checked.

"I smell good to myself," I said.

I looked up my sleeve. There was a blob of lingonberry jam in my armpit.

19

MRS. LEE CALLS. AGAIN.

When I heard my dad yell, "Hello, family," I raced
downstairs.

"You're dripping wet, Adam," my mom said.
"And you're in your underwear."

"I jumped out of the shower when I heard Dad.
Having you home is the only good thing about today."

"Thanks, Sport. Now run up and get dressed."

Due to my supersonic eardrums, I could hear my
parents from upstairs.

"He showered but it still smells bad in here," my
mom said. "I think it's time to get him deodorant."

Hot diggity dog! I'm getting deodorant!

"We'll pick some up at Grubb's drugstore, on our way to Mrs. Lee's," my dad said.

"She called you at work again?" my mom said. "About what?"

That's what I want to know.

Facts about Mrs. Lee:

1. She blames Sam and me for everything bad that happens on Capitol Hill except when it's the government's fault. Then she blames my dad.
2. She blames her dog for nothing.
3. She is a bigger tattler than Ashley.

I sat on the top step until my dad called me.

To put him in a jolly mood I said, "What's up, Rhino Butt?"

"Nothing good," he said. "If I'm to believe Mrs. Lee."

"Don't. She is a worldwide exaggerator," I said.

"She said you let Mitzi out," my dad said.

"It was more like Mitzi let herself out," I said.

"She unlatched the gate?" my dad asked.

"No. She chased me up the fence. I had to grab on to the gate to save myself."

"You were on the sidewalk and Mitzi fenced you?" my dad asked.

"Not exactly. I was in her yard."

"I'm not understanding," my dad said.

"It was ninety-six degrees. I had to cut through to drink out of their hose," I said. "You know what Mom says about me getting dehydrated."

"How far did Mitzi get?" my dad asked.

"She ran across the alley, under the fence, and into the Golds' yard. I had to climb their super-high fence. By the time I got over, Mitzi had dug up a load of flowers. I was putting them back and Mitzi, for no reason at all, tried to bite my elbow."

"That dog is aggressive," my mom said.

"Let's walk over to the Lees', Sport. You need to make an in-person apology."

"I know, Personal Responsibility," I said.

My mom told my dad, "Tell Mrs. Lee it's a miracle Adam still has his toes."

"Most gerbils weigh more than Mitzi," my dad said. "I don't think our boy was in danger."

"She's five pounds," I said.

"Four of those pounds are teeth," my mom said. "That dog is high-strung and a menace to children."

"That's what I've been telling you, Mom. Mrs. Lee is anti-children."

"Mrs. Lee is high-strung and she's certainly quick to blame others, but she's not a menace to children," my mom said.

On the way over, I told my dad about Lucy Rose.

"When I'm mad at Sam or he's mad at me, we say, 'Cut it out.' Or the mad one socks the other one in the arm. Then it's over," I said.

"Females do not respond well to arm socking," my dad said.

"It's not a hard punch," I said. "It's a sock in the arm, like when you see a Volkswagen Beetle and shout, 'Punch buggy, no punch back.' Girls play that too."

"Did you apologize?"

"Lucy Rose rejected it," I said. "Mom said I should write a note."

"Good idea," he said.

"Figuring out the ways of girls and ladies is a task," I said.

I told Mrs. Lee I was sorry about Mitzi. "Luckily, my elbow is only scratched," I said.

She didn't forgive me either.

I never knew how long it takes to pick a deodorant. My dad said he likes unscented.

"What's the point of that?" I said. "Nobody will know you're wearing it."

"They'll know if I'm not wearing it," he said.

"It's between Old Spice and that one with the neon lightning on it," I said.

"Old Spice is for a mature man," my dad said.

"Then that's the one for me," I told him.

20

EVEN WORSE

"Betty," my dad called. "We're back. Why are the lights out?"

"Make your way to the dining room and sit down," she said.

I felt my way along the wall.

"Ta-dah!" my mom said.

"Whoa! I never knew we could do sparklers in the house," I said.

"You can't," my mom said. "These are special Adults Only indoor sparklers from Hill's Kitchen."

When the sparklers fizzled, my dad flipped the light switch.

"Presenting Mount Vesuvius!" my mom said.

I could not believe it. She was holding a shining hump. It was wiggling. The bottom was yellow. The middle was Creamsicle color. The top looked like strawberry milk shake. Globs of light purple were oozing out of the top. Dark green lettuce was sticking out of the bottom.

"Betty, in the forty-two years I have been alive, I have *never* seen anything like this," my dad said.

Nobody has.

"I'm not surprised," my mom said. "Mount Vesuvius is an all-day project. I don't imagine many people have the patience to make it."

"It reminds me of Jell-O," I said.

"I used powdered gelatin so I could make my own colors."

"It's tilting like the Leaning Mountain of Vesuvius," I said. "But don't worry. I'll save it." My finger poked through the Creamsicle.

"Don't touch," my mom said. "It's fragile."

"I'm guessing it's flavored," my dad said.

"The recipe says the yellow layer tastes like corn pudding," my mom said. "Only without cream and with gelatin."

"Why are there blood spots in it?" I asked.

"Really, Adam," my mom said. "Those are beet balls. The color seeps, that's all. The middle is full of mandarin oranges, shredded carrots, coconut, and a super food called chia. The remarkable thing is that in muffins chia tastes like crunchy seeds. But put it in liquid and it turns to gel."

"Double gel," my dad said. "How about that?"

"The peak is made of gelatin mixed with tomato juice," my mom said. "It's called aspic. I think it has an interesting flavor."

I think the person who invented aspic should be arrested.

"What's the lava made out of?" my dad asked.

"Low-fat mayo and a little purple food coloring," my mom said. "Bernice Bombono is a fan of mayonnaise."

"Isn't gelatin see-through?" my dad asked.

"Not when it's mixed with Neufchâtel cheese,"

my mom said. "If it were transparent, my next surprise would be ruined."

My mom put the mount on the table and picked up the pie cutter. "Adam, do you want to start with one color or stripes?"

"I can't choose," I said.

She stabbed the point, cut down like it was a watermelon, and pulled out a jiggling triangle. Lumpy gunk poured out.

"That's the molten core!" my mom said. "It's really cottage cheese with food dye."

"It looks like blue throw-up," I said. "Sorry, I meant to think it, not say it."

"What?" my mom asked.

My dad gave me an unpleasant look. "He said he'd like to grow up," my dad told her.

"Nothing encourages growth more than vegetables," my mom said.

"What are the green bits floating in the yellow stripe?" my dad asked.

"Emeralds," my mom said.

"Emeralds?" I said.

"Bernice Bombono says kids respond to treasure,"

she said. "You tell them to use their forks to excavate precious jewels."

"Why would kids want to eat precious jewels?" I asked.

"That's a good question, Sport."

"Bernice Bombono is a professional author," my mom said. "She knows things. Besides, they are really broccoli."

The mountain tour kept going. "The brown specks in the orange layer are walnuts," she said.

"They look like stinkbugs," I said. For some reason they thought that was an insult.

"The yellow chunks are pineapple," my mom said.

The doorbell rang.

My dad answered.

"Come in, Pop!" he said.

"Madam and her pals went strawberry picking," Pop said. "They got carried away. So she loaded our Radio Flyer and sent me out to make deliveries. I can't go home until it's empty."

I leapt up. "Pop, is Lucy Rose still mad at me?" I asked.

"Her feelings are wounded," Pop said.

"I wrote her a letter," I said.

"Do you want me to drop it off on my way home?" Pop asked.

"Yes," I said.

"We'd love some berries," my mom said. "The Melons are all about health these days."

"I heard," Pop said.

"Join us for supper," my mom said.

Run for your life, Pop.

He put a basket of berries on the table. "They're washed and ready to eat," he said.

"Have a boulder of Mount Vesuvius," I said.

Pop studied every side. "I'm afraid anyone who sees this will find the real Mount Vesuvius in Italy to be a sad disappointment."

"Help yourself, Pop," I said. "Take a ton. Two tons."

"If only I had room," Pop said. "Madam and I had chicken curry for supper and a great many strawberries."

I speared through the goo and pulled out some tangled carrot shreds. They tasted okay once I sucked off the lava.

"Don't overlook the beets, DB," my mom said.

I never wanted not to eat something as much as I did not want to eat a beet.

"Sorry, Mom," I said, "but I can't think of one good thing about beets."

"Vitamins," my mom said.

"I don't think about vitamins," I said.

Pop leaned over and whispered in my ear.

"Are you sure?" I asked.

"If you are one of the lucky ones," Pop said.

"Dad, pile on the beets," I said.

"I'd like to be that convincing," my dad said.

I took a bite. "They taste kind of like dirt."

"Oh, dear," my mom said.

"I don't mind," I said. "People eat around five pounds of actual dirt in their lives. Plus about seventy-seven insects. And those are the ones they didn't mean to eat."

Mom gasped. "Have you eaten an insect on purpose?"

"It was a long time ago," I told her.

"And yet he won't eat eggplant," my dad said.

I avoided the lava and the molten core. Luckily, when you tip your head back, gelatin slithers down your throat.

To make my mom feel appreciated I ate the emeralds. Compared to the rest of Mount V, broccoli is five-star food.

"I'd better get back to my strawberry route," Pop said.

At the door, my mom said, "Pop, does our house smell okay?"

He nodded.

My mom said he was being polite.

Pop left with my letter in his pocket and a paper plate covered with a tinfoil tent.

"Put it in the wagon, Pop," I whispered. "Mount Vesuvius probably can eat through paper."

After dinner I lay down on the dining room floor. I could hear my parents loading the dishwasher.

"I hoped we'd have Mount Vesuvius left over for tomorrow's supper," my mom said. "But Adam gave Pop a rather large piece."

"Adam can have the rest," my dad said. "We'll have something simple."

My mom made a ladyish laugh. "Excellent idea."

"You know, Betty," my dad said, "I'm surprised that a woman who loves French food and gourmet restaurants would suddenly develop a taste for gelatin volcanoes."

"You shouldn't be," my mom said. "Adam loves my creations and I love Adam. I'm thrilled that he's finally eating vegetables. And his gratitude touches my heart."

"You are a mom among moms," my dad said.

"Get used to it," she said. "We'll be eating cars and volcanoes until our Darling Boy goes to college."

"Noooo!" my dad said. It sounded like a moan.

That was when I realized the tragedy. When I dumped the yacht in the furnace and fooled my mom into thinking I loved it, I tricked her into ruining my childhood.

21

WHY I LOVE BEETS

I called Pop first thing.

He didn't answer, so I had to keep calling until he answered. The old don't always hear on the first try.

"Hello, Melonhead," he said.

"Pop!" I said.

"It's six-fifteen in the morning," Pop said.

"I know," I said. "I'm calling to tell you I'm one of the lucky ones!"

"One of the fourteen percent?" Pop asked.

"Yes!" I said. "I just found out!"

"Congratulations!" Pop said.

I could hear Madam in the background.

"Congratulations for what?" she was asking.

"I'll let Melonhead tell you himself," Pop said.

"What's the news?" Madam asked.

"Are you sitting down?" I asked.

"I'm lying down, actually," she said.

"Even better in case you faint," I told her. "Because guess what? When I eat beets my pee turns red!"

"You must be very proud," Madam said.

"Anybody would be," I told her.

When I came back upstairs my parents were standing in the hall.

"What's on your mouth?" my mom asked.

"Probably beets," I said. "I fished them out of Mount V and ate them for breakfast."

My mom hugged me until my feet didn't touch the floor.

"How about that?" my dad said.

Then he turned to my mom. "Betty, I still don't smell anything."

"Inhale," my mom said.

"Question," my dad said. "When you think the milk has turned sour, you tell me to taste it. When you think something smells, you tell me to find the cause. Why is that?"

My mom laughed. "That's the way marriage works," she said. "I am the one who sounds the alarm. You are the search party."

"Can I help?" I asked. "I like finding stink."

My dad put on his shorts and a Frager's Hardware T-shirt.

"Get your nose, Sport," he said. "We don't have much time before school. We'll start in the basement."

"You know, Dad, when I finish college we could have a smell-finding business," I said. "Our truck would say Melon and Melonhead."

"Check the washing machine," my dad said. "Forgotten clothes can be a mega-stinker."

"It's empty."

My dad reached up and felt the pipes.

"Dry as sand," he said.

We checked under the sink and outside the drain, then the main floor and the top. Also my sneakers and my dad's gym bag.

"What a complete disappointment," I said.

"Don't paint the truck yet," he said.

My mom was in the backyard eating diet yogurt and picking off dead flowers.

"Did you find it?" she asked. "You checked every room?"

"Betty," my dad said. "I don't smell anything peculiar. We've gone from cellar to attic. I'm afraid the smell is in your head."

"I agree," my mom said. "It's in the nose part of my head."

"Your sense of smell must be sharper than mine," he said.

"Or maybe I'm going nuts," she said.

22

THE GRAY DAY

Sam and I knocked on Lucy Rose's door.

Nothing.

"Knock again, Glenn," Sam said.

It opened.

"Hello, boys," Lucy Rose's mom said. "The girls left for school ten minutes ago."

I couldn't believe it.

"Without us?"

"I'm afraid so," she said.

"Did Pop give Lucy Rose my letter?" I asked.

"He did," she said.

Sam and I turned around.

"Keep trying," her mom said. "You have a good friendship."

"This stinks, Sphinx," I said.

At least Pip had waited.

I told her the Lucy Rose problem.

"I feel bad," Pip said.

"It's not your fault," Sam said.

"I would have happily given her my unicorn head," Pip said.

That made me laugh.

"Did you finish your MAFDP?" Pip asked.

"I haven't even found out who I admire," I said.

"I'm doing Leo Gerstenzang," Pip said. "Inventor of Q-tips."

"He's your most admired dead person?" I said.

"I can't decide whom I most admire," she said. "But Q-tips are popular and I feel sorry for Leo Gerstenzang. Everybody goes for Galileo and Leonardo da Vinci and those guys. Nobody writes about Leo."

*   *   *

When Lucy Rose saw me on the playground she looked away. Pip waved. I'm not sure if Lucy Rose saw her.

During geography Ms. Mad came over to Pip's desk.

"Pip, you look a bit pale. Do you feel all right?" she asked.

"I have a small headache," Pip said.

"Go to the nurse," Ms. Mad said.

"I don't need to," Pip said. "It'll go away."

"I never pass up that offer," I whispered.

For the rest of the day Ms. Mad was Pip's personal Hovercraft.

"She's stuck on you like poo on a shoe," I whispered to Pip.

Pip snorted.

At lunch Pip complained, "Ms. Mad keeps saying, 'Can I get you anything?'"

"I'd say, 'A chocolate milk shake and an iguana, please,'" I told her.

"Enjoy the easy life," Sam said.

"Easy lives are not exciting," Pip said. Then she backed up, did a one-eighty, and rolled across the room.

"She's at Lucy Rose and Jonique's table," Sam told me.

"What are they saying?" I asked Sam.

"Who knows?" he said.

After lunch I passed Lucy Rose a note. Nothing came back.

But at language arts I got a message I didn't expect.

Dear Mr. Melon,

Thank you for your interest in the Vegalicious! Lifestyle for Children. I do hope you will also enjoy *Very Vegalicious! Making Food Even More Fun,* coming out next spring. Children everywhere are sure to enjoy my newest creation, Some More S'mores! The secret: tofumallows! Be sure and pass the good word—VEGALICIOUS! Your friends will thank you.

Sincerely,

Bernice Bombono

The split second I read it, I answered.

Dear Mrs. Bombono,
   Did you read my letter? I do NOT like
you. You have ruined my life! Plus you made
me do something I'd rather not mention. You
should take Personal Responsibility. You are
an adult, after all.

                    Adam (Melonhead) Melon

P.S. You are not dear to me. That is just an
expression you have to use when you write a
letter.

After recess Ms. Mad told Jonique to collect the
language arts homework.
   Pip said, "I didn't do it."
   Ms. Mad walked over to her and talked softly.
But my desk is two feet away. I tuned in with my
supersonic hearing.
   "Bring it tomorrow, Pip," Ms. Mad said.
   Bart's homework was lost.

"NO excuses," Ms. Mad told him. "Report to the Reflecting Table after school."

We worked on our Animals of the Rain Forest maps until the bell rang. Ms. Mad said Pip could skip the assignment if her head was still hurting.

I could tell Pip was mad, but her butterflies came out great. Sam's python looked a little real.

My stick insect looked like sticks. "My problem is the legs end up being twigs," I told Ms. Mad.

"Excuse me, Ms. Madison," Pip said. "You have a smudge on your face."

"Thanks for the heads-up, Pip."

"Is heads-up a joke?" I asked.

"An accidental one," Ms. Mad said.

"It's near your eyebrow," Pip said.

"Here?" Ms. Mad said.

"The other one."

Ms. Mad rubbed her forehead with her hand.

"Higher," Pip said.

"Is it gone now?" Ms. Mad asked.

Pip got a wad of Kleenex out of the secret arm compartment in her chair.

"I'll wipe it off for you," Pip said.

"Thank you, Pip," Ms. Mad said.

She bent down so Pip could scrub her forehead.

"Done," Pip said.

"Thank you. Ten more minutes, cartographers!"

Ms. Madison straightened up. Her entire forehead was dark gray.

Laughing broke out. Mine came out of my nose.

"You are the jolliest class I've ever had!" Ms. Mad said.

Pip was smiling. When no one was watching she opened the tissue and showed me.

Crushed artist's charcoal! Pip is a genius.

Ms. Mad had to say "Let's settle down" eleven times.

Nobody settled.

But here is the amazing part: NOBODY told Ms. Mad that her forehead was gray. Not even

Ashley. Maybe because Pip let her off personal servant duty.

"Kathleen, please collect the maps," Ms. Mad said. "Pierra, you may hang them on the classroom clothesline. The rest of you are as jumpy as fleas. Shake your arms, exhale, and calm down. Mr. Pitt is coming to spend the last ten minutes of the day with us."

Mr. Pitt looked like he always looks. Short hair, short-sleeved shirt, short tie. I know zip about clothes but I doubt he is a Man of Style.

"Good afternoon, Ms. Madison," Mr. Pitt said.

She said, "Hello, Mr. Pitt," but she didn't look up. I could tell she doesn't like him because her face was pink. Except for her forehead, I mean.

"Hello, fifth graders," Mr. Pitt said.

Then he put up a sign that said There Is No *I* in *Team*.

"A first grader knows that," Ashley said.

"After we talk about teamwork, we'll have time to dialogue," Mr. Pitt said.

Whatever that is.

I did not even know I was tipping my chair backward until I saw Hannah's upside-down face.

Ms. Mad's head bounced up.

"Adam," she said. "How many times is this going
to happen?"

"I don't know," I said.

"Mr. Pitt, please continue," Ms. Mad said.

He did not. He stared.

"Gail—er, Ms. Madison, what happened to your
forehead?"

"Nothing," she said. "Why?"

"It's gray," he said.

"My forehead is gray?" she said.

"Gray," Mr. Pitt said.

The whole class was laughing like loony chim-
panzees.

Ms. Mad took a circle
mirror out of her drawer
and clicked it open.

Then she said, "Pip, I
will see you at the Reflecting Table after school. Plan
to stay for a half hour."

"I can't," Pip said. "I have a class at three-thirty."

"In this class there are NO excuses," Ms. Mad said.

I never saw anybody so happy about being punished.

Even though Ms. Mad was mad, everybody got to check for email from their interesting person.

"I haven't even gotten one and Melonhead got two," Ashley said. "Unfair."

"The president gets thousands of emails," Ms. Mad said. "He may not have the time to answer each one."

I read mine.

Dear Mr. Melon,

Thank you for your interest in the Vegalicious! Lifestyle for Children. I do hope you will also enjoy *Very Vegalicious! Making Food Even More Fun,* coming out next spring. Children everywhere are sure to enjoy my newest creation, Some More S'mores! The secret to their success: tofu-mallows!

Be sure and pass along the good word—
VEGALICIOUS! Your friends will thank you.
Sincerely,
Bernice Bombono

Mrs. Bombono,
You sent me the same letter twice. It has not changed my mind. I still think you are a bad influence on children.
Adam (Melonhead) Melon

P.S. Getting a letter from an author isn't all it's cracked up to be. In fact, it is annoying.

23

IT'S GETTING WORSE

Our doorbell rang at eight a.m.

"I'll get it," I said.

"DB, let's not have company this early," my mom said. "Saturday morning is my lazy time. I'm still in my robe."

"It's not company, Mom. It's Sam."

"It kind of stinks in here," Sam said.

For a tired person my mom can move fast.

"Sam, please, do *not* tell anyone our house smells."

"It's interesting news," he said.

"No, Sam. Not even your mom. Or dad," she said.

Sam shrugged. "Okay."

"He respects the Cone," I said.

"Of Silence," Sam said.

"Thank you," my mom said. "This is an embarrassing situation."

"Ha!" I said. "Sam and I aren't the only ones who get in situations!"

My dad came downstairs. "All the closets smell like is mothballs," he said.

"That smell turns my nostrils," I said.

"It's an improvement over the smell we've got," my mom said.

"Now I must say that the guest room smells a little," he said. "Adam's room smells like it usually does."

"I never thought I'd be glad to hear that," my mom said.

"The only thing I found were footprints," my dad said.

My mom hugged herself. "What kind of footprints?" she said. "Where are they?"

"On the wall. Dozens, all in a horizontal line. They're about that size." He pointed at my feet. "Get the sponge and the cleaning spray, Sport."

I never mind jobs that use spray.

"While we're upstairs we'll check Mom's workroom and the bathrooms again," I said. "Sam and I know a ton about common scents from being Junior Special Agents."

It didn't take long.

"Come up here!" I hollered. "Mom's study smells really gross."

"Like what?"

"Chemicals," Sam said.

"Mixed with grapefruit rinds, and that flower vine Mom can't stand."

My mom stopped on the stairs.

"Those are my smells, DB. I put grapefruit drops on the lightbulb, Odor-B-Gon on the furniture and curtains. I spritzed the rugs with the honeysuckle perfume Grandma gave me. All that was supposed to fix the smell."

"It didn't work," I said.

"I think the smell is fading," my dad said.

"I'm turning off the air-conditioning and opening the windows. I don't care how hot it is," my mom said.

"Good idea, Betty," my dad said. "All we have to do is keep our cool. I'll keep mine at the office. I've got to help write the congressman's speech to the Sierra Club."

It seems to me that the person saying the speech should be the writer of it.

"I'll be out getting a haircut and running errands," my mom said.

"Sam and I have a load of outside stuff to do," I said.

Due to my mom's overreaction to stink, Sam and I got to eat breakfast at Baking Divas.

"Three Hamwiches, please," I said. "We need added energy today."

"I'm scared to see you boys with added energy," Aunt Frankie said.

"Can we have all the free water we want?" Sam asked.

"Help yourself," Mrs. McBee said. "Fill 'em up."

Here's what we did:

> Rode our bikes to the Air and
> Space Museum.
>> Sweated.
>> Practiced hand-walking.
> Sweated.
Squirted each other with the hose.
Gave Julia a dog bath.
>> I got sent home. Sam washed
>> the mud off his sister with squirt-
> ing soap.
>> Sweated.

"Mrs. Alswang, can Sam still spend
the night at my house?"

She stopped scrubbing Baby Julia's dress.

"I wouldn't have it any other way," she said.
"Sam will be over when his chores are done. The
first one is hosing down the steps before someone

breaks their neck slipping on all that dish-washing soap."

"If I help, the work will go twice as fast," I said.

"That scheme did not end well last time," Mrs. Alswang said.

"I'll be quick, Slick," Sam said.

"See you then, Ben."

24

P-U x 2

My mom was sitting on our front steps. She was speed-breathing. That's clue number one that she's in panic mode. She was fanning herself with a pizza delivery advertisement.

"Don't panic!" she said. "I've called Daddy at work."

"I'm not panicked," I said.

"You should be," she said. "The smell has taken over. It has engulfed our house. Daddy found a company that specializes in getting rid of unwanted pests and odors, but the person can't get here until Monday afternoon."

I hooted. "I can't wait for two days for someone to get here."

"Me either," my mom said.

"I've always wanted to meet a professional stink finder," I said.

"What if it's permanent?" my mom said. "What if they can't find it? Or fix it? What if we have to live in a smelly house forever?"

"Calm down, Mom," I said. "You know my motto: Trouble Isn't Permanent."

"Sometimes it is," she said. "When you jumped off Sam's bunk bed your tooth didn't grow back."

"Don't worry. They'll find the smell. Probably an animal got trapped behind the wall and died."

She started breathing double-fast. "A mouse!"

"A dead mouse couldn't make that big a stink," I said. "It's something bigger. Maybe a possum."

My mother made the sound called wretching. It comes from feeling wretched.

"We are leaving this house of horrors," she said.

"Where are we going?"

"To the library. Later, we'll meet Daddy at the

Taverna. If it isn't raining, we'll come home and sleep on the back porch. If it rains, I guess we'll stay at the Capitol Hill Suites hotel."

Thanks, smell!

Her face got droopier.

"I was going to make Bernice Bombono's Never-Fail Sticky Broccoli for supper. The book says it tastes like candied apples, only it's broccoli."

"I've had too many treats," I said.

"It makes me happy to hear you call vegetables a treat," she said. "Who would think one book could turn around a child so fast?"

Backfired.

"Do you need anything from inside?" my mom asked. "Most Admired is due Monday."

The day after tomorrow?! I'm on the fast train to trouble.

"I'll get my notebook," I said.

"Are you scared to be by yourself with the moldering possum?"

"Why would I be?"

She was too upset to answer.

"Mom, relax. Enjoy being outside."

"It's ninety-five degrees and about to rain," she said.

"Want me to shut the windows?" I asked.

"You are a thoughtful boy," she said. "When you're done, turn the air-conditioning back on. Cool, dry smelly is better than hot, wet smelly. Then grab your Most Admired report and come out."

Mentioning the undone-report situation will turn bad into worse.

My mom made a shaky half-curve smile.

"Are you sweating or crying?" I asked.

"Mostly sweating," she said.

"Don't you worry, Mom. I have everything under control," I said. "E-Z P-Z."

I opened the front door and stood in the vestibule.

"So far, it's only a middling stink," I yelled.

My mom perked up.

"Opening the vestibule door," I hollered.

I jumped back. "Whoa, no!" I screamed. "Gag-o-matic!"

For smell control I

jammed my index and middle fingers up my nose. I ran up the stairs. Even with my nose plugged, the smell stuck to the back of my throat.

I talked myself through the job.

First stop, parents' room.

Fingers out. Slam window. Fingers in. Repeat until all upstairs windows are shut.

For speed I did my one-handed backward banister slide to the first floor.

Living room windows shut.

Kitchen. Put chair against swinging door so it will stay open. Howl when knee hits chair.

Windows slammed.

Composition book found.

Turn on air conditioner thermostat.

Run.

I heard hissing behind me.

For a second I thought I was under possum attack. Then I remembered it was the air conditioner turn-on noise.

Shut the windows.

One was stuck open. I grabbed the top, picked up my legs, and swung.

It crashed down so fast my knees hit the wood floor. My face smacked flat on the heating vent.

Why is cold air coming out of the furnace?

Holy moly! I ran around the house like the fastest cheetah in Africa.

Sit. Think.

I plopped down on the radiator.

And all of a sudden, my brain shifted and I had the worst thought ever.

Please be wrong.

My eyes landed on my mom's homemade Guidelines for Life poster. Personal Responsibility is a top GFL. I felt like throwing up. Not from the stink.

I did the only thing I could think of. I called Pop. I tried acting like I was just wondering, but Pop can figure me out.

"Tell me the problem," he said.

"I can't," I told him. "It's in the family Cone of Silence."

"The family Cone is important," Pop said.

"I need you to explain one thing. Really fast."

When he finished I called Sam and screamed, "Top-level Red Alert! Meet me at the Southeast Public Library, near Reptiles."

My mom doesn't like that section, so it's like a Privacy Zone.

I ran out the front door.

"Ready, Mom?" I asked.

"Never readier," she said. "We're making a quick stop at Congress Market on the way."

"Are we buying more smell remover?" I asked.

"No," she said. "I'm buying my brave boy the biggest treat they sell."

I wanted Twizzlers but I picked a honey bun to punish myself.

25

A STRESSFUL SITUATION

By the time we got to the library, I had been rained on so much my underwear was wet.

Sam was sitting on the floor between the shelves, dripping on a foldout about how to hatch crocodile eggs.

"What's the emergency?" he asked.

"I found the stink," I said.

"What's the cause?"

"A car, a yacht, and a unicorn," I said.

Sam gasped. "Are you sure?"

"Completely," I said. "Smell my breath. My tonsils are coated with stink. Plus, I shined my flashlight down the vent."

"What did you see?" Sam asked.

"A lumpy pinkish-gray pile with long white hairs. Next to that is a wave of green moss with puffy black patches. It's going up the walls, overlapping something shiny that looks like yellow Vaseline," I said.

"Cool!" Sam said.

"It's Bacteria City. The Tower of Mold."

"How big?"

"Huge. The bottom of the duct is covered. It might have been growing before my eyes."

"How come it didn't get burned up?" Sam said.

"How come I forgot we had radiators?" I said.

"Everybody on Capitol Hill has radiators," Sam said. "What's the problem with that?"

"Radiators have pipes," I said. "Not vents."

"We should have shoved the food down a pipe?" Sam said.

"No," I said. "Going by what Pop said, it would be impossible."

"You called Pop?" he asked.

"He said the furnace heats the water tank and turns it into steam. The water, not the tank. The steam goes in the radiator and makes it hot, then it cools down and turns back into water and recycles back into steam."

"But the vent still connects to the furnace, right?" Sam said.

"The vent connects to the air-conditioning," I said.

"I have personally been in houses that have vents with heat pouring out," Sam said.

"Loads of houses are like that," I said. "Except for ancient ones like ours."

"Don't blame yourself," Sam said. "Probably heating professionals can't tell the difference between heat vents and air-conditioning vents. Not right off the bat."

"I am mad at myself," I said.

"Don't worry. All we have to do is kill the Tower of Mold," Sam said.

"Before the stink professional comes on Monday," I said.

"Otherwise, we're fried toast," Sam said.

"This is worse than when we invented butter balloons."

"Worse than the garbage can whirlpool experiment," Sam said.

"We have to fix it tonight, after my parents are asleep."

"How?" Sam asked.

"No idea," I said.

"Pop says Lucy Rose is a natural-born problem solver," Sam said. "We should call her."

"I did. She won't answer," I said.

I heard my mom whisper-yelling. "Adam. Where are you? Have you finished your Most Admired?"

"I haven't found an MAFDP," I whispered to Sam.

"How about Harry Coover, inventor of superglue?" Sam said.

"He's probably my mom's MAFDP," I said. "Plenty of things get busted in our house."

"Ditto," Sam said.

"My mom wants to go to a restaurant but she didn't say you could come," I said.

"That's okay," he said. "I'll meet you at your house in two hours."

I left him in Reptiles and walked behind the racks. I came out by a display of books for romantic people.

I said cheerful things to my mom all the way to the Taverna Restaurant. They helped one percent.

My dad was waiting.

He hugged my mom.

"You're damp," he said.

"It rained earlier," she told him. "We were in it."

"Bad luck," my dad said.

"Yes, but it was the best luck I had all day," she said.

She sat on my dad's side of the booth. He put his arm around her shoulder.

"The smell is so much worse than anything you can imagine," she said.

Get her thinking it's not so terrible.

"Dad can imagine worse," I said. "I admit it's not a great smell but what about kitty litter boxes?"

"Let's not dwell on kitty litter, Sport," he said. "Mom's stomach is a fragile organ."

"Whoo—ooo—whooo," I said.

They sat there.

"Get it? I was being an organ," I said. "Like in a scary movie or church."

"Sorry, Sport," my dad said. "This is a stressful situation for all of us."

"Not for me," I said. "I don't care if we never get rid of the smell."

My mom closed her eyes.

"We will get rid of it, Betty. Of course we will."

"Thanks to the smell, we're having our first family campout," I said.

My mom put her face in her hands.

"Betty, we'll go to a hotel if you'd rather," my dad said.

"They're so expensive," my mom said. "And who knows how much it will cost to get a dead possum out of the wall."

"What makes you think there's a dead anything behind our wall?" my dad asked. "And why a possum?"

"It could be a raccoon," she said. "They have thumbs."

My dad turned her head toward him and looked her in the eyeballs. "Betty," he said. "I don't know what's making the smell, but I know it's not a raccoon, dead or alive."

"You are not a raccoon expert," she said.

"I'm sure the Alswangs or the McBees would put us up for the night," my dad said.

NO!

"I will die if Lola McBee finds out that we're having a smell problem," my mom said. "She keeps a spotless house. And if the Alswangs find out, they'll never let Sam come over again."

"Sam's sleeping over tonight anyway. Remember?" I said.

"No," they both said at once.

"You already said he could," I said.

Supersonic message to Dad: Please, please, please times infinity, say yes. You must say yes.

"I'll ask the Alswangs if you can spend the night there, Darling Boy."

"Sam can camp on the porch with us. Stink doesn't bother Sam. He likes it. Ask him."

When the waiter asked me, "Fries or salad?" my mom said salad.

I wanted to say, "Haven't vegetables caused enough problems in our lives?"

"Extra beets, please," I said. "And, Mom, even if the Alswangs find out—"

"Which they won't," my dad said.

"Baby Julia has caused so many toilet overflows, the Alswangs don't judge other people's smells."

My parents are anti-begging but I had to do it. Curing the vent situation was a two-man job.

"I'll trade dessert for Sam," I said.

"Are you scared to sleep outside, DB?" my mom said.

"No," I said.

My mom looked at my dad. I knew her supersonic message to my Dad was *Adam's frightened but he doesn't want to admit it.*

"Mom," I said.

I stopped.

Scared is good!

I made my bottom lip shake.

"If Sam wants to stay over, he may," my dad said. "But if he changes his mind, I won't be the person walking him home at midnight."

"He won't change," I said. "Sam is a friend you can count on."

When my dad paid, he said dinner was pricey. For some reason, I felt like it was my fault that we had to eat expensive food.

26

THE GREAT SOLUTION

My dad went to the third floor to get pillows, blankets, my sleeping bag, and flashlights. We changed in the basement with the door open for air. My mom wore shorts and a T-shirt. She didn't want the neighbors seeing her pajamas.

"It doesn't smell as much here, does it?" my mom asked.

"It's hard to tell," my dad said. "I think my nose hairs are singed."

Sam's dad dropped him off.

"That's a big bag for one overnight," my dad said.

"Thank you," Sam said.

"Let's roll out the sleeping bags."

"Time to sleep," I said.

"It's eight-thirty," my dad said.

"Let's have a sing-along," my mom said. "When I was a girl we had them all the time."

She started with "This Old Man" and went straight into "Little Rabbit Foo-Foo," which is immature for a two-year-old.

I yawned at the top of my lungs.

"Ready for 'She'll Be Comin' Round the Mountain'?" my mom asked.

Supersonic message to Sam: What will force them to fall asleep?

"How about 'One Hundred Bottles of Beer on the Wall,' Mrs. Melon?" Sam asked.

That is a proven method.

"You are too young to be singing about beer," my mom said.

"Let's lie on our backs and look for bats," I said.

"Bats?" my mom said. "We have bats?"

"Remember? I told you there are thousands of bats on Capitol Hill," I said. "They fly in swarms."

"We can't sleep outside," my mom said. "They could attack us."

"Betty," my dad said. "We will not get bitten by bats."

"They could be circling right now, looking for human flesh," she said.

"No, they're not, Mom," I said. "Vampires are a myth."

Sam and I lay on top of our sleeping bags on the porch.

"No talking," I whispered.

It took over two hours for my parents to stop reading and turn off the porch light. We had to wait for my dad's snores to get to level ten.

Sam whispered in my mom's ear, "Melonhead hasn't started his biography."

"Don't risk my neck any more than it's already risked," I said.

"Sorry, Atari. We needed a surefire test," he said. "If she heard that, her eyes would have flipped open."

"Since your suitcase has the supplies, hoist it

on your back and crawl toward the kitchen door,"
I said.

"Silent mode," Sam said.

The back door creaked when we opened it.

"Freeze!" I said.

No parent moved.

I rolled across the tile floor to the scissors
drawer.

"Take your T-shirt off," I said. "Tie the armholes
into knots. Cut eyeholes. Then pull the shirt down
to your forehead."

"Like my head is wearing a skirt?" Sam asked.

"It's called a face curtain," I said. "It's a stink
blocker. I just invented it."

In the dining room I pulled off the vent cover.
Sam shined the flashlight down the hole.

"Wowee-pizowee! The Tower of Mold is an awe-
some monstrosity," Sam said. "It's
sad that we can't leave it there
forever."

"It's grown since this afternoon," I said. "Two more days
and it would climb through

the vent and become the mold that ate the dining room."

"I would love to see that," Sam said.

"Who wouldn't?" I asked.

"Your parents," Sam said.

"Ready to duct dive?"

"Hold my ankles," Sam said. "I'll scoop up the goo with my hands."

His head went down easy but he was stopped by his shoulders.

"The vent seemed bigger when we were tossing dinner," Sam said.

"Incoming brainstorm," I said. "We duct tape a mop to my ankle. I drop my leg down the chute and swing it around."

"E-Z P-Z," Sam said. "I brought tape."

I went to get the mop and came out with a better idea.

"A vacuum?" Sam said.

"Put the round furry brush on the end of the silver tube," I said. "You lower it. I'll hold the hose and shine the flashlight on the mold. You guide the sucker."

We lay on our stomachs.

"One glob slurped up," Sam said. "It looked exactly like snot."

"Superfine, Einstein," I said. "Five minutes from now we'll be back on our sleeping bags, eating Popsicles and talking about how we saved my house."

Clunk.

Sam looked down. "Did you know vacuums come apart?"

"Yes. But I didn't think this one would."

"Luckily only half of the silver tube fell off. Plus the brush," he said. "Even if we can't get it, your mom can still vacuum. She'll just have to walk on her knees."

"Don't you worry," I said. "We're inventors."

The solution hit my brain like balls of hail.

"Raid the refrigerator!" I said.

We came back with a load of magnets. Two said From Your Friends at the National Orange Growers' Association, one Washington Nats magnet, one shaped like Florida, three that came free with

Dee-Lite-Full Yogurt, a flat-faced cat, a fake flower, and one I Heart My Son. "I gave that to my mom for Mother's Day," I said. "Be careful with the red high-heel magnet. Aunt Traci gave it to my mom."

"Two Buddy Boyd for Congress magnets," Sam said.

"He looks older in person," I said. "Believe me."

"One World's Best Dad," Sam said.

"I gave my dad that for Christmas," I said.

"Snap," Sam said. "I gave my dad the exact same thing for Hanukkah. What are the chances of that?"

"It's like we have the same mind," I said.

"Now we let the magnets do the dirty work," I said. "Right before our very eyes my mom's ordinary Swiffer sweeper is becoming a Rescue and Recovery System."

I yanked off the Swiffer cloth. "I'll hold the mopping end steady, Sam. You wrap duct tape around it, sticky side out."

"I just figured out how duct tape got its name," Sam said.

"We stick the picture sides to the tape so the magnets will have maximum pickup power," I said.

"Man-o-man. What a machine," Sam said. "Only it's too short to reach the bottom of the Tower of Mold."

"Simply simple," I said. "Duct tape the Swiffer handle to my mom's broom. Automatic extender."

To make it touch bottom I had to lie on my side with my arm and shoulder in the vent.

"Sam, you're the eyes of this operation. Guide me."

"A little more toward me," he said. "The magnets are pretty near the vacuum tube. Try twirling the Swiffer."

"My armpit circulation is getting cut off," I said.

"Are we sure the vacuum tube is magnetic?" Sam asked.

"Not one hundred percent."

Fwap–fwap–slap-p-p–fwap–splat.

"Raise the broom," Sam said. "I'll shine the light on the tower."

"Oh, no, no, no!" I said. "We didn't catch the

tube—the vent caught the magnets! They're stuck to the sides! Buddy Boyd's head is in the red high heel, and he's about to get hit by a Florida orange."

"The other Buddy is upside down," Sam said. "What went wrong?"

"Metal beat tape," I said. "The magnets peeled off and jumped onto the metal."

"Maybe mold steam weakened the tape," Sam said.

I was going to say we should give up, but then I thought. "Remember when we were at Mei Wah restaurant and Mr. La taught us how to use chopsticks?"

"You are a brilliant genius!" Sam said. "All we have to find is a pair of giant chopsticks."

"You know the bamboo poles my mom uses in the yard?" I said. "They're in the basement. Creep down. Get two. I'll go upstairs."

He got back first.

"I found rubber bands in my mom's office," I said. "Here's the fattest paperback book I could find. It's so old it's from when my dad was in college."

"What's an *Iliad*?"

"Who knows?" I said. "I read enough to figure out it's not important."

Sam held the bamboo. "Put *Iliad* in between sticks," I said. "I'll tie rubber bands to hold them together."

"We each operate one stick," Sam said.

"Pinch it open. Get one stick on each side. Let it snap shut like giant tongs."

We practiced picking up my mom's gardening hat.

"It's easier with real chopsticks," Sam said.

"We're going in," I said.

"Quit banging the sides. Your parents will hear," Sam said.

"Shine the flashlight straight," I said.

"You try aiming with your armpit."

"Give it to me," I said. "I'll hold it with my teeth."

"Move!" Sam said. "Stop! We're over the vacuum. Unpinch."

Sploosh.

"I forgot the flashlight was in my mouth," I said.

"At least we can look at the bright sides," Sam said. "Get it? Bright sides of the vent."

"The light really bounces off the mold," I said. "It's beautiful."

"It's hypnotizing me to sleep," Sam said.

I held up my glow-in-the-dark watch. "We're sleepy because it's four-forty-four in the morning."

"The tower is collapsing," Sam said.

"Or spreading."

"Can mold melt flashlights?" Sam asked. "Because plastic could smother the mold."

"That's it! Seal off the vent! With no oxygen the mold will starve and shrivel up. I think."

We used a roll of Saran wrap and the rest of the duct tape.

"That smell is trapped," Sam said.

"Open the windows," Sam added. "We'll spin dishtowels like helicopter propellers. Fan the leftover stink out of the house."

We sat down to enjoy our success.

27

TROUBLE X INFINITY

The next thing I heard was shrieking. "The boys! They've been knocked out by the smell! Toxic gas!"

I woke up.

"Mom!"

"Adam!" my mom said.

"Sam!" my dad said.

"Where am I?" Sam said.

"The gas gave him amnesia," my mom said.

She moved from me to Sam.

"It's Mrs. Melon, Sam. You're okay. Can you sit up?"

He bounced up so fast his head hit my mom's chin.

"The boys are fine, Betty," my dad said.

"Smell!" my mom said. "It's a little better."

"You're right, Betty," my dad said. "Why don't you go back to bed? It's early. Or should I say 'go back to porch'?"

"Worry exhausts me," she said.

"You've had plenty to worry about," he said.

He waited until the back door shut. Then he said, "Let's sit at the table."

"I'd like to go home now," Sam said.

"I'd like to know why the air-conditioning vent is glowing," my dad said.

"There's a flashlight in there," I said.

"Why?" Sometimes he gets a tone.

"Blame Bernice Bombono," I said.

It took a half hour to explain.

"I do not see this situation as Mrs. Bombono's problem," my dad said. "This is about Personal Responsibility and Consequences."

I wanted to say, "We are taking a load of Personal Responsibility by leaving Pip out of the story." But I didn't, because then we wouldn't be.

"This is not like the time we did the stink bombs behind the funeral home," I said.

"That was back when we had trouble with our judgment," Sam said.

"You told Mom you ate your dinner," my dad said.

"We didn't say that. Mom did."

"Take the plastic off the vent," my dad said.

"It looks bad down there," I said. "But don't worry. While you were talking I figured out how to get it out. All we need is Mom's hoe from the backyard."

"Why a hoe?" my dad asked.

"There's not enough room in the vent for a shovel to scoop," I said. "But a hoe is like a small bulldozer. All we have to do is load, raise, and dump."

"Or we could use the wet vac," my dad said.

"Vaccums don't work for this," I said.

"How do you know that?" he asked.

It bugs me when grown-ups ask a question when they know they will not like the answer.

"The wet vac is made for things like this," my dad said.

"Moldy food in ducts?" Sam said. "I thought we were the first people with this problem."

My dad grabbed the best parts of the job. Sam was in charge of making sure the wet vac stayed plugged in. I had to hold the trash bag.

"Tomorrow we'll have the professionals steam clean the vents," he said.

"You know how you always say boys will be boys, Dad? When you think about it, this is kind of a no harm, no foul situation," I said.

"This was a case of boys being knuckleheads," my dad said. "You have to tell Mom."

"It will kill her feelings," I said.

"That's one consequence," he said.

"Do you want your wife to be sad?" I asked.

"No, but honesty is part of the Code of the Melons," he said.

When he says that, I feel like I have to do it.

"Your mom says that if we get in a situation, she wants to hear it from you instead of an M.O.T.H." Sam said.

"Or Mrs. Lee," I said.

"Or Mrs. Wilkins," Sam said. "Or Mr. Neenobber."

"Mom's outside, Sport," my dad said. "Sam, drop this bag of mold in our garbage can on your way home."

"I'm going home?" Sam said.

"And, Sam," my dad said. "We're going to have to let your mom and dad know about this. They might prefer to hear it from you first."

"Good thinking, Mr. Melon."

I woke my mom up by bringing her coffee on the back porch.

"Made fresh by me while Dad was in the shower," I said.

"I didn't know you knew how to brew coffee, DB."

"Nothing to it," I said.

My mom took a sip.

"Oh, my," she said. "This is tasty."

"No offense, Mom, but you

should brush your teeth. They're covered with brown specks."

"How did you make the coffee?" she asked.

"I microwaved a mug of water, stirred in coffee, and added milk," I said. "E-Z P-Z. It's good, right?"

She nodded and took the cup from him.

"I dread going back in the house," she said.

"Don't you worry," I said. "The smell's almost gone. It turned out to be coming from the air-conditioning vents."

"That explains why it was in every room in the house," she said. "Every time the air conditioner turned on, the smell traveled around through the ducts."

I nodded.

"What was causing it?" she asked.

"Umm," I said.

"A dead raccoon! I knew it!" she said.

"Not a raccoon," I said.

"A possum?" she said.

"Don't start breathing, Mom," I said.

"Big or small?" she asked.

"It started off small," I said. "It got bigger."

"A possum grew in our vent?"

"It's over now," I said. "Exhale."

"You are the bravest boy I ever met," she said.

Twenty more layers of guilt fell on me.

"It was food," I said. "It spoiled."

"Possum food?" my mom asked.

"There are no animals in this story," I said. "People food."

"I am so confused," my mom said. "How did food get in the air-conditioning system?"

"We put it there," I admitted. "And we are sorry. We thought it would just catch fire and burn up."

"There was a fire?" my mom said.

"No fire. Just food."

"*What food?*" my mom said. "And why did you put it in the vent?"

"Thecaryachtunicorn," I said.

"I can't understand when you're mumbling," she said.

"The car," I said. "The yacht. And the unicorn. We are completely sorry we disrespected your work."

My mom's mouth flopped open in that shocked way.

"But you loved your yacht," my mom said. "Why would you drop it through the vent?"

I felt like I had a knot inside my neck.

"We thought the duct connected to the furnace," I said.

"I understand that part. But why did you want to burn dinners that you loved?" she asked.

"Because we didn't," I said.

"You didn't?"

"Didn't like it," I said.

"Pip liked her unicorn," my mom said. "Right?"

"No." I said it as quietly as I could.

Her eyes bugged out. "Pip threw her unicorn down the duct?"

I nodded.

"I was wrong about her," my mom said. "She is a terrible influence."

"It was my idea, Mom. Pip just went along with it."

I tried to think of one good thing.

"She liked the look of it," I said. "It was crafty. Like it could be in a book."

"It was in a book," my mom said. "That's how I got the idea."

"We didn't want to hurt your feelings," I said. "And who would believe kids over Bernice Bombono anyway?"

"Mount Vesuvius?" my mom said.

"Artistic," I said. "And historical."

"This is a blow," my mom said.

I thought she was going to yell. She was silent.

"Want me to bring you some yogurt?" I asked.

She didn't say.

"I'll pick a good one," I told her.

My dad was in the kitchen.

"How'd it go, Sport?"

"Not well at all," I said. "She looked like she was feeling stunning."

My dad laughed.

"She is stunning," he said. "Do you mean she looked stunned?"

"Aren't you stunning when you're stunned?"

"Stunning means gorgeous," he said.

"Who knew that?" I said. "Not me."

I got the yogurt called Crème de la Crème Coconut Pie and went back outside.

She ate a spoonful.

"Pop called your Bernice Bombono food a triumph," I said.

"He did like Mount Vesuvius," my mom said. "It helps to remember that."

"He said the triumph was that you love me so much you spent hours making food for my health even though it's not your taste," I said.

"Or yours," she said.

"My triumph was I pretended I loved it because I love you so much."

"Pop said that?" my mom asked.

"Yep," I said.

"Is he right?"

"Yep."

It took her a long time to finish the C de la C.

Finally, she said, "I love you so much that I said I loved the coffee you made. But after you went inside I poured it over the railing."

"Are you saying that to make me feel good?" I asked.

"I dumped it," she said. "But I had the good sense not to dump it in the air-conditioning vent."

"You're older," I said. "You know things."

Then she Heimlich hugged me.

"Are you still upset?" I asked.

"Yes," she said. "But you're still my DB."

"I'm going to tell Dad that I faced my consequence," I said.

"Tell him you faced one consequence," my mom said. "This particular incident will have several. Daddy and I will have to decide what they are."

One of my chores was to return Sam's suitcase. He was watching Baby Julia while Mrs. Alswang wrote thank-you notes.

Sam put a plate of milk on the kitchen floor and said, "Here you go, Fifi." Julia put her face in it.

"I'm in mega-trouble," he said. "I have to

apologize for bad judgment. Plus, I'm giving your parents my future money to help pay for the duct cleaner."

"Ditto," I said.

Due to paying for a different incident, Sam and I are out of savings.

I tied a piece of string to Julia's dress strap and walked her around the kitchen while Sam read a comic.

"I'm going the long way home," I said.

"Past Lucy Rose's?" Sam asked.

"Just in case she's done with being mad at me," I said.

Julia curled up on the welcome mat. Her legs were bent under her stomach and her bottom was up in the air. She was licking her arm.

"Are you sleepy, dog?" I asked.

"Meeyowl," Julia said.

Then she curled her fingers and scratched my leg. Hard.

28
A GOOD THING

Lucy Rose was hula hooping in her front yard.

"Hi," I said.

"Hey," she said.

"Did Sam tell you what happened?" I asked.

"He told Pop. Pop told me you two created the Leaning Tower of Mold."

"Sam and I spent all night trying to get it out," I said.

"You should have borrowed Pop's wet vac," she said.

"I knew you would know what to do," I said. "I wish you'd answered the phone."

"Sorry," she said.

"Are you still mad?" I asked.

"No," she said. "Madam says we are not the type of people who complain about not being invited. Even when our feelings are shattered to pieces and bits. Also, I don't care if Pip is your friend, because she's my friend too. She came over all day yesterday. So did Jonique."

"What did you do?"

"We finished our MAFDP biographies and went to the flea market. I bought a change purse that looks like a panda. Then we went to Baking Divas. Mrs. McBee just invented Ginger Snappy Ice Cream Sandwiches. We got the first three ever sold—or not sold, because we got them for free since we were Jonique's guests."

"I haven't done my MAFDP yet," I said. "I don't even have a dead person."

"It's due tomorrow," she said.

"I know. I'll have to sit at the Reflecting Table for a month."

"I'll be back in a minute," Lucy Rose said.

When she came out she handed me a piece of paper.

"What's Le Pétomane?"

"Look it up," she said. "I can't do every living thing for you, Melonhead."

29

LE PÉTOMANE

The footpool met in front of Jimmy T's.

Sam gave me a piece of folded toast. "It's got honey on both sides," he said.

"Here's a clementine," Jonique said.

"Thank you, lady and gentleman," I told them. "Who wants to hear today's news?"

"The Scoop du Jour," Lucy Rose said.

"My mom is rejecting Bernice Bombono's Vegetable Lifestyle," I said. "Today I had eggs and a sausage biscuit and raw carrots for breakfast."

"You don't eat carrots," Jonique said.

"I do now," I said. "Once you eat Mount

Vesuvius, the vegetables you used to spit out taste pretty good."

"How did it go at the Reflecting Table on Friday?" Sam asked Pip.

"I stayed an extra fifteen minutes."

"You got in more trouble?" I said.

"No. Ms. Mad and I had a chat. She said she was disappointed in me for making her look ridiculous in front of the class and Mr. Pitt. I said I was sorry. Then she asked me why I did it."

"What did you tell her?" Sam asked.

"The truth. I said, 'To get you to treat me like a regular kid.'"

"She was utterly shocked to her inner bones," Lucy Rose said. "Jonique and I already heard the story."

"Ms. Mad said she's never had a student with my special needs before. I said my special need is a wheelchair, which I already have. Then she said I should tell her if I need anything."

"What did you say?" I asked.

"'I need a chocolate milk shake and an iguana.'"

I hooted.

"Not really," Pip said. "I told her I'd like to be able to go upstairs. She said she'll get me a key to the teachers' elevator."

"You can take us on rides," Sam said.

"I had to promise that I wouldn't," Pip said. "Then Ms. Mad said she was sorry. Then she said I taught the teacher some things and that coloring her forehead was a creative solution."

"You get away with everything," I said.

"*But* that if I ever pull a stunt like that again, the Reflecting Table will become my permanent desk."

"She's not Bad Ms. Mad," Jonique said. "More like Firm Ms. Mad."

"Who wants to be the first to read their Most Admired Person in History report?" Ms. Mad asked.

For the first time ever I waved my hand more than Ashley. "Pick me," I said.

Ms. Mad did. I walked to the front and read.

My Most Admired Famous Dead Person:
Joseph Pujol
By A. H. Melon
Grade 5

There are a lot of admirable dead people in the world, but to me the greatest is the excellent French entertainer named Joseph Pujol. He was also known as Le Pétomane, which is French for The Fartomaniac.

It was like a laughing machine exploded in Room Nine.

"I beg your pardon," Ms. Mad said. "I didn't hear the translation correctly."

"Fartomaniac," I said. "Le Pétomane was also called a fartiste."

The class laughed harder. Bart Bigelow stamped his feet.

"Adam," Ms. Mad said. "Return to your seat. This assignment is not a joke."

"Neither is the fartiste," I said. "In the 1890s he was the best-paid entertainer in France. He made a load more than some famous actress named Sarah Bernhardt. He did his act in the same theater called Moulin Rouge."

"That is the most unfortunate translation I have ever heard," Ms. Mad said. "But sometimes what sounds like one thing in one language means something quite different in another language. What was Mr. Pujol's talent?"

"Farting," I said. "May I finish reading?"

"If I find out that you made this up, I will not be amused," Ms. Mad said.

I started again.

Le Pétomane had the gift of being able to fart anytime, every time. Every night he would stand on the stage and make every kind of fart you can dream up. He did musical farts that sounded like trombones. He farted the French national anthem. He did farts that sounded like animals. And he could play the flute with his butt. People laughed so much that the Moulin Rouge had to have nurses standing around to help people who fell out of their chairs. At the end of the show he blew out candles by farting on them.

The tragedy of his life was that he died in 1945.

After school Sam walked me home so if my mom had heard the good news about my grade, she'd treat us to something delicious at Baking Divas. But when we got home and took off our shoes on the rug where we always left them, Mom's were missing.

"She's not home, Gnome," I said.

"Bad deal, Carrot Peel."

I topped him with "You're vegalicious, Aloysius."

"Call your dad," Sam said. "He's probably waiting next to the phone."

It turned out he was waiting in a meeting.

"Daddy-O!" I yelled.

"What's up, Sport?"

"Remember you said Bart Bigelow should get another skill because there is no job for a boy with his talents? Boy, were you wrong."

"I was?" he said.

"In France, people get paid to fart," I said. "Well, they did in the olden days. And farts are still hilarious today."

My mother came in the back door right after I finished explaining.

"Did you tell Mom about the fartiste?" my dad asked.

"Not yet," I said. "She doesn't even know I got an A on my MAFDP!"

"Let her glory in your grade before you tell her the topic," he said.

My mom dropped her trowel and hugged me off my feet. She yelled into the phone, "Did you hear that? DB got an A! An A! What a first impression!"

She switched back to me. "Invite the Alswangs and choose the menu, Adam! Vegetables can take the night off!"

"No way!" I said. "Sam and I want beans."

"And beets," Sam said.

I have heard about people jumping from joy but this was the first time I saw it happen. My mom hugged Sam and me so hard our heads banged. She fell down on her knees.

"I can't believe it!" she said. "An A and you are asking for vegetables! Two of my fondest dreams came true at the same time! Can life get any more perfect?"

"Much more," I said. "After dinner, Sam and I are going to do a performance that will truly surprise you."

"You know," my mom said, "Daddy was right. Kids really do mature in the fifth grade."

STRONG BODY! SHARP BRAIN!

You and your friends and family can go to this E-Z P-Z website to learn more about what you should eat to stay healthy and have lots of energy!

ABOUT THE AUTHOR

Katy Kelly used a number of vegetable-disappearing maneuvers as a kid. She has since learned to love most veggies, which have made her a sharp-eyed, hilarious adult. But due to an unfortunate childhood dinner, she will never enjoy brussels sprouts. This is her eighth book for young readers and the fourth in the Melonhead series.

ABOUT THE ILLUSTRATOR

Gillian Johnson has been sneaking vegetables into her family's dinners for a while now, but (shhh!) don't tell them—she wants to continue her tried-and-true methods.